One Sword, One Soul

ANDREA BIRCH

authorHOUSE®

AuthorHouse™
1663 Liberty Drive
Bloomington, IN 47403
www.authorhouse.com
Phone: 1-800-839-8640

First published by AuthorHouse   11/04/2011

ISBN: 978-1-4567-8601-4 (sc)
ISBN: 978-1-4567-8602-1 (ebk)

Printed in the United States of America

Any people depicted in stock imagery provided by Thinkstock are models,
and such images are being used for illustrative purposes only.
Certain stock imagery © Thinkstock.

This book is printed on acid-free paper.

Chapter 1

Saying Goodbye

In the 21st century there are people who still train with swords, this is Anna's story.

As I was leaving the South Palace, a picture on the wall caught my eye.

"Do you remember that day?" I jumped, as I heard the familiar voice, I turned my body around to where the voice had come from.

"Oh you scared me Jai." I said to the Prince. But he kept walking towards me as if I hadn't interrupted him. "You looked really beautiful in that dress, and with that brown hair tied up, and those hazel eyes are gorgeous." I felt my cheeks burning, but I was not sure if he had noticed. "Are you making a compliment Prince Jai?"

"Yes Anna." The Prince said.

I was that close to him that I could feel his warm breath against my face. As I looked into his brown eyes, I leaned in and kissed him on the cheek very swiftly. I turned away from him and said "Bye Your Highness." I walked outside to where Dean was waiting for me. As I walked away from the palace of the South with Dean, I turned to look at him to ask him a question, when King Jou's daughter ran up and called out to me.

"Anna!" I stopped and spun around Dean did the same.

"Princess Mia." I said and dropped down on one knee as she ran towards us. Princess Mia is Prince Jai's six year old sister, as she ran up to towards us; her long black hair flowed out behind her. When she got closer she came to a stop and looked at me, her face was saddened.

"Anna, please don't go away."

"I have to go away Princess, it hurts me to leave but I have to obey your father's order."

I noticed a tear fell down the Princess's face; I wiped it off for her.

The Princess murmured "Dean look after her please."

Dean knelt down beside me and whispered to the Princess with great courage in his voice. "Anything for you my Princess."

"Princess, can you do me favour?" I asked her.

"Yes, Anna, of course I will." The Princess said.

"Can you look after Snowbell for me?"

At that moment Snowbell came running up towards me, I picked Snowbell up and hugged her, then handed her to the Princess, the Princess put Snowbell on the ground. I said bye to the Princess.

The Princess said "Bye Anna, bye Dean."

I got up and Princess Mia wrapped her arms around my legs. I put my hand lightly on her shoulder. "I have to go now Princess."

I took my hand away from her shoulder and she stepped back. I too took a step back and Dean and I turned around at the same time and started heading towards where our horses were waiting for us. As we set off on the dirt road to the north region we went over a wooden bridge which wasn't very far away from the south palace. I asked Dean some questions about my new master.

"Is he a good trainer?"

Dean replied with a smile. "Yes of course he is the best in the north region anyway, by the way Anna, his name is Kayato."

I replied with a smile. "Okay."

Looking around at the countryside there I could see the hills. About an hour on horseback, all of a sudden we came to a stop. I looked at Dean and he looked at me. I looked to the right side of me, and there was a house.

"That's Kayato's house." Dean informed me.

"It's beautiful." I replied. The house had a veranda out the front and two guards out by the front door.

As we made our way to Kayato's house, I took in everything that was around me at this point. We stopped a few feet away from the steps of the veranda and got off our horses. The first guard stepped forward and introduced himself;

"Hello, my name is Shi-Lou."

Dean stepped forward and introduced himself to Shi-Lou; "Nice to meet you, Shi-Lou, my name is Dean." And then gestured to me. "This is Anna."

"Hello Anna." Shi-Lou said.

The other guard stepped forward to introduce himself as well. He wasn't quite as tall as Shi-Lou.

"Hello, my name is Jin."

"Nice to meet you Jin." Dean and I said. *This Kayato must be rich to have two guards.*

"Please, follow me; Jin will take care of your horses." Shi-Lou said.

As Dean, Shi-Lou and I walked towards the front door, Shi-Lou opened it, Dean and I walked in and I noticed the house was fairly big inside. When we first walked through the door there was a hallway, Shi-Lou lead us around a corner and then we were in the lounge room. As Shi-Lou suddenly stopped and Dean came to a sudden stop too, I too slowly stopped behind Dean. I noticed that Shi-Lou was standing in line with Dean. I took a slight step forward so that I was in line with Dean and Shi-Lou. Then I saw them, all four of them, standing side by side, with a little girl standing in front of her parents she looks about the same age as Princess Mia. The little girl smiled, and I couldn't help myself but smile back at her. The oldest male stepped forward, his black hair and dark brown eyes stood out against his clothes, he wore a white kimono.

"My name is Kayato, and this is my wife Yasumi."

I noticed that Kayato's voice sounded Cantonese. His wife then stepped forward with a little smile, but kept in line with him.

"This is our son, Taro."

As I looked at him before he stepped forward I noticed that the young woman, who was standing next to him, was holding his hand. *This must be his girlfriend.* As Taro took a step forward like his parents had done, the young woman dropped her hand, and he let go of her hand also. He smiled then looked at Kayato, and Kayato lightly put his hands on the shoulders of the little girl who standing in front of him, and said:

"This is our daughter Monikku."

She looked at Dean and me. Then Taro started to speak and gestured to the young woman beside him. "This is Emika."

She also stepped forward, her long hair tied up in a high pony tail, she also smiled, and I guessed that she was nervous as much as I was.

Beside me I heard Dean take a step forward, I decided it was best if I stay where I was, Dean once again introduced himself, once he had finished he stepped back to where Shi-Lou and I were standing. I then took a step and also introduced myself. Monikku's eyes lit up as I said what my name was. After Dean and I introduced ourselves to Kayato and his family, Shi-Lou went. I guess he went back to his job guarding the house.

Yasumi, still in the same position said softly. "Come, I will show you to your bedrooms, and the rest of the house."

Yasumi led us down another hallway, on the left hand side the door was slightly opened, Yasumi stopped in front of the door I noticed that her kimono was a cream colour, which suited against her skin. She walked into the bedroom, we followed her in. The bedroom was fairly big, there was a window on the side wall and the bed was a single queen bed, next to the bed was a brown wooden bedside table with a lamp on it. Then at the foot of the bed I saw my luggage.

"Your luggage came a couple minutes before you arrived here." Yasumi told us.

We kept walking down the hallway and on the right side of the hallway there was another door that was slightly opened, we walked in and I saw Dean's luggage was at the foot of the bed. The bed in this room was a double king sized bed and the room was also a bit bigger.

"I hope the bedrooms are to your liking." Yasumi said.

"Yes, thank you." Dean and I said at the same time.

"The bathroom is just to your left." Yasumi informed us.

I noticed that when Yasumi spoke her voice was quiet soft. It reminded me of how my Mother would speak. We made our way back into the lounge room, and I didn't noticed this the first time I walked into the house, but the lounge room and kitchen were joined, there was a big arch door between the two rooms. We stepped outside onto another veranda, this veranda had two small circular tables and wooden chairs, even though there was a bigger table inside they must sometimes eat meals out here. There was a stone wall, not very high only eight stones tall, and there was a garden around some of it, I also noticed that some of the stones were out more than others, they were like seats. And I saw the horse stables on the right hand side of the garden, probably about one hundred meters away from the garden.

Yasumi then turned to us and lightly said. "Please feel free to have a rest; you must be tired from the journey."

"I do feel a little tired." I said and walked back into the house and down the hallway to the first bedroom door that was still slightly opened. As I walked in I took off my sword and sat it down in its case that had came with my luggage, the beautiful silver handle on it made it easy to find when I had misplaced it. I lied down and closed my eyes.

It felt like I had only been asleep for five minutes, but it must had of been longer, it was now dark outside my window.

I put my sword back on and walked out in to the hallway, I could hear Dean's voice, it was coming from the kitchen, and I walked out to the lounge room. Dean and Kayato were sitting at the kitchen table.

"Did you sleep well?" Kayato asked me as I stopped walking.

"Yes I did, Ka—" I thought I better not say his name yet, he didn't say to me to call him Master Kayato or just Kayato. He looked up from the table and looked at me.

A smile came onto his face. "Please call me Kayato."

"Okay" I smiled back, "Do you mind if I go outside? I need some fresh air."

"If you want to you can." He said.

"Thank you." I lightly said.

"By the way Anna, dinner will be ready soon." Dean said.

"Okay, I won't be long outside."

I opened the door, and closed it behind me without looking, I looked at the roof, and there were lanterns. I walked down the steps and on to the grass, as I made my way over to the stone wall I could still hear Dean and Kayato talking in the kitchen. As I sat down on stone wall and rested my back slightly against the wall I heard a noise. Just then a person leapt over the stone wall. *Was this a test?* I quickly withdrew my sword, and stood in a fighting stance. The person had black clothing on, and walked towards me, as I moved my sword into an upward strike.

The person stopped and said "Anna, it's me, May-Lyn."

"May-Lyn!" I nearly shouted her name.

"Hey Anna."

"What are you doing here, how did you know I was here?" I quizzed her.

She sat down on the stone wall, and I sat beside her. Her black hair had grown since the last time I saw her, her brown eyes stood out against her black clothing.

"Well you see, I asked around if anyone had seen you and a couple of people said that you were headed to Kayato's. I wanted to make sure you were okay, that's what friends do. Oh and I kind of borrowed my father's horse." She said.

"So you borrowed your father's horse without asking him first, right?"

"Yeah but ay listen, if the North officers come here tomorrow and ask you any questions about my whereabouts, lie to them."

"What! You want me to lie. May you know what happens when I lie, I start to get panicky and if I get found out that I lied, I'll be arrested."

"You'll be fine, just tell them I have gone west. I'm actually going to the east; I need to sort out some business. So what are you doing out here in the fresh night air?" she said calmly.

"I fell asleep, and woke up with a headache." I replied bluntly.

"Oh." She said.

Just then I heard another noise.

"It's okay Anna, it's only Jiro." May-Lyn said.

He then jumped over the wall, but different to the way that May-Lyn jumped over the wall, he put his hand on top of the wall and pushed down and jumped over the wall. He also wore a black kimono but without the belt. His short black hair stood out against his tanned skin and his brown eyes.

"Hi Anna." He said in his light tone voice.

"Hey Jiro." I said with a smile on my face. Then the horses on the other side of wall started making a noise.

"I don't mean to interrupt, but May we better go." Jiro said quietly.

"Okay." May replied. We both stood up at the same time, I turned to face her, and she hugged me tightly.

"May, I can't breathe." I said breathlessly.

"Oh, sorry Anna." She said in her quiet voice.

"It was nice to see you again Anna." Jiro said.

"Same to you Jiro." I said. Then May-Lyn and Jiro walked to the wall holding hands, and climbed over it.

I noticed movement on the back veranda out of the corner of my eye, when I fully turned around to see who or what it was, nothing was there. *Mm I wonder what that was.* I thought to myself as I made my way back up to house, as I walked back into kitchen. Kayato was sitting at the head of the table, Dean was sitting on Kayato's right hand side; and Yasumi was sitting on Kayato's left hand side. They were eating dinner as I walked in.

"Would you like some dinner?" Yasumi's soft voice said.

I moved my right hand so it was on my left sleeve and lightly rubbed my right hand up the sleeve. I noticed that Kayato was looking at something. "No thank you, I have a headache, I might go to bed."

Yasumi smiled and nodded.

As I walked down the hallway and came to the first door, I walked in and went to my suitcase and unpacked my belongings and put some of my clothes in the wardrobe. I put my sword in its case, and grabbed my night clothes and also my toiletry bag and went to bathroom.

After I had a shower and cleaned my teeth I kept my toiletry bag in the bathroom and I went back to my bedroom and pulled the covers back and got in, I got comfy and took off my locket that was around my neck and put it in my hand and opened it, I looked at the picture it held of my parents, my mother with darkish blonde hair and hazel eyes and my father with his brown hair and brown eyes, as I lied down in bed, I started to think about them, and I missed them, and I cried myself to sleep.

The next morning I fell out of bed, and then I remembered my locket, I looked on the floor and then on the bed, and then I looked at the bedside table, and there was the gold locket, sitting on the table, it was shut. I got up off of the wooden floor and grabbed my light pink kimono, my sword and also my locket and went to the bathroom. After I got changed and put my locket on, I put my night kimono on my bed and walked to the kitchen. They were all sitting at the table eating breakfast, but Kayato wasn't there, I looked outside and saw him in a sitting position and eyes closed, meditation.

"Do you want some breakfast, Anna?" Yasumi's voice came from the chair she sat in.

"Yes please."

I sat down between Dean and Monikku. After breakfast Dean and I went outside to where Kayato was doing his meditation. He got up from his position and smiled at us. I wasn't really paying attention, I was thinking about Prince Jai, and how much I missed him. Kayato stood with his hands in front of him, "Good morning, to both of you."

"Same to you." Dean said.

"Good morning Kayato." I said.

"Today we're just going to do basic training." He said.

I nodded. As he withdrew his sword, I notice that he was already standing in fighting stance. I quickly withdrew my sword. All of sudden he came at me, he brought his sword up into a striking position, well that's I thought he was doing, I tried blocking the upward strike, but he moved the position of his sword so it was just above his waist and came at me. I gasped and took a step back, he repositioned his sword so the tip of the sword was pointing straight at me, again he came at me, but this time I blocked his move as well as took the tip of the sword off. I looked at the tip, and then looked at Kayato. He just stood there looking at me. A few feet behind me, I heard Dean slightly move.

"Well done Anna." Kayato said.

Before I could say thank you, he came at me again, this time I blocked his move and he blocked mine, the training session lasted about an hour. As I was catching my breath, Yasumi brought out two glasses of water. I grabbed one glass and took a sip of water; Kayato looked past me and then walked up the steps to inside.

Chapter 2

The Visits

As I took another sip of my water, I heard footsteps; three other people joined Kayato as he walked down the steps into the garden, where Dean and I were still standing Kayato stopped walking, but the other three kept walking, which were officers from the North region I could tell they were North officers because they were dressed in light blue, around the collar and sleeves were dark blue, they stopped walking and turned to face me. They were all male, the older officer was at the head, and the two younger officers were at his flanks. The head officer had black hair and brown eyes. He kind of reminded me of May-Lyn's father, Daichi.

"Good morning to all of you." Said the head officer.

I started to panic, but told myself to *stay calm and answer whatever questions they have for me and also lie for my best friend.*

"We're here on business. We would like to know the whereabouts of the Princess of the North region is. She has stolen her father's horse." He said.

The Princess I thought to myself. "Who is the Princess?" I asked, and then I decide to take another sip of water, rather a gulp then a sip.

"Please, take a sip of water, don't mind us." Said one of the younger officers.

I took a gulp of water when the head officer started to speak again.

"Princess May-Lyn." He said.

I got such a shock that I spat out the water that was in my mouth. "So sorry, I didn't mean to do that." I said in embarrassment.

"That's okay" The officer said. "We want to know where the Princess is." He said calmly.

"Where the Princess is, I heard Jiro said that she went west." I said nervously, my heart started to race, the head officer glared at me, it scared me and it was like they could hear my heart pounding.

"Thank you, did Jiro say why May-Lyn took her father's horse?"

"No, he didn't say why, although I do have a question." I said calmly. "What will happen when they find her?"

"She might be put in the North castle jail." The head officer answered my question.

I nodded and kept a straight face and I said to the officers. "I have to get back to my practise."

I put my glass down on the ground near a stump. Kayato showed the officers out and the three of them left and headed west just like I was hoping, I didn't want to lie to them but I didn't want to let my best friend down. I felt conflicted did I do the right thing or the wrong thing? Time can only tell. I then ran to the horse stables and quickly saddled my horse.

"Where are you going?" Dean shouted as I went down the dirt road towards my grandparent's house.

"To my Grandparents." I shouted back.

"Kayato is not going to like this when he finds out." He said.

"I'll deal with that later." I shouted back.

When I finally got to my grandparents, which was thirty minutes away from Kayato's house. I thought of something. *I wonder why May-Lyn never told me that she is a Princess.* As I reached the front veranda of my grandparents house Genichi their house guard welcomed me when I got off my horse.

"Hello Anna." He said through his smile.

"Hello Genichi" I answered him, also with a smile. "Is Grandma home?" I asked.

"Yes she is." He said.

I smiled and walked in to the kitchen "Grandma." I said lightly, she had her back to me, but then turned to face me.

"Anna sweetheart." She said to me as she walked towards me.

She smiled and I smiled, she squeezed me, her hazel eyes looked at me.

"Please have a seat." She said.

We sat down at the kitchen table; I put my hands on the big wooden table. I sighed.

"What's wrong Anna?" She said to me.

"Well I just found out that my best friend is a Princess, and I lied to the north officers about her whereabouts. I lightly said "But she visited me at Kayato's house last night and told me she was going to the east to sort out some business but to tell the officers that she went west." I sighed "Did you know that I am being trained by Kayato now?" I said remembering that she probably didn't know that.

"You know how word travels around these parts, sweetie, is he a good trainer?"

"Yeah he is." I guess she saw the sadness in my eyes.

"How are you coping?" She said as she lightly grabbed my right hand squeezed it.

"I'm coping fine, but I will not believe my parents are dead, they can't be" I said. "And you, how are you coping?"

"I've been better, your Grandfather barely speaks to me anymore all he does is spend time at the stables and then comes and eat when it is time to eat and then he goes to sleep. I haven't seen him this bad since we moved from Australia that took a lot out of him."

"Would you like me to speak to him, maybe he will talk to me."

She smiled at me still squeezing my hand. "Would you, if you're not too busy with your training." She said a little more happily.

"No I'm not too busy with training." I said, well it wasn't a lie, because we only had one training session this morning.

She squeezed my hand one more time and I smiled at her, she smiled her little smile, then she looked outside, I turned my head to where she was looking. Uh oh, Kayato was coming along on his horse. *Dean must have told him where I got to, of course he would of, and because when he probably got back to the garden and didn't see that I was there he asked Dean where I had gone.*

I started to play with my hair, now I was really panicky.

Grandma looked at me. "anything the matter Anna?"

"No, nothing is wrong at all; I'll go and see Grandpa now."
I said.

"Okay." She lightly said to me.

As I made my way out from the kitchen onto the veranda
and down the steps Kayato was just getting there, as he
stopped he jumped of his horse, I noticed that Genichi took
his sword out.

"Genichi, it's okay." I told him.

He nodded and put his sword away. As I lightly made my
way up to Kayato, he just stood there looking it Genichi
and then he looked at me but didn't say anything.

"I use to be a good kid; I did what I was told, but that all
changed a month ago so look, if you want to yell at me,
punish me or whatever it can wait till we get back to your
place." I nearly yelled what I said.

Once again he just stood there looking at me.

"Now if you don't mind, I would like to see my Grandfather,
Genichi please show Master Kayato inside." I said more
calmly.

I walked to my left and kept walking, and then I saw it. The
sword that I stuck in the ground, when Dean told me that
my parents were dead, even though it was a month since
their death, I still remember it like it was yesterday, it was
raining that day.

Not very far away from the house I heard Grandma introduced herself to Kayato. "Hello, it's nice to meet you my name is Marree."

"It's nice to meet you, my name is Kayato." He said in his Cantonese accent.

As I kept walking, I saw the horse stable and my Grandpa at one of the horse gates patting the brown thoroughbred. "Grandpa." I said lightly.

He turned around, his white hair under his brown hat, he walked up to me. "There's my favourite granddaughter." He said with a smile.

"Grandpa, I'm your only grandchild." I said with a smile.

"And that's why you're my favourite." He smiled and ruffled my hair, as we walked back to the house he put his arm around my back, and pulled me close.

"So what brings you here on this fine day?" He asked me.

"I just wanted to see you and Grandma; I haven't seen you for a while." I answered him.

"True." He said.

"Grandpa, my new master is here."

"Yes, what about him?" He asked.

"I thought I'd better warn you before we got into the kitchen." I said as I looked at the house.

As we made our way to the house, Genichi greeted us as we got to the front veranda; Grandpa took his arm away from my back. We walked in, and Grandpa took off his hat and sat next to Grandma, and I sat down next to Kayato. I just looked at the table I placed my hands on the table and put my hands together.

"Hello my name is Jeffery." Grandpa introduced himself to Kayato.

"Nice to meet you Jeffery, I'm Kayato."

Just then Kayato looked past the kitchen. I looked up from the table and saw Diego, his big body with his beautiful grey hair walking towards Kayato.

"That's just Diego." Grandpa said.

"And he is a Tamaskan dog." Grandma assured Kayato.

Diego walked up to Kayato and stopped and looked at him, Kayato looked at Diego, Kayato put his left hand down beside him, Diego went up to his hand and sniffed Kayato's hand. Diego then sat down, but lifted one paw and put it in Kayato's hand.

"He wants to shake hands with you." I said quietly still looking at the table.

Kayato turned his head slightly to face me and nodded then he focused back on Diego, and shook his paw. After this, Diego walked towards me, I patted his grey fur and he took the pink sleeve of my kimono in his teeth and tugged on it, I got up and Diego led me to the side door of the kitchen that led to outside.

"Hang on Diego" I said. "Is it okay if I go outside with Diego?" I asked Kayato, he nodded.

Outside I could hear the three of them talking, as I picked up a stick and threw it as far away for Diego as I could so I could secretly listen to what my Grandparents and Kayato were talking about, I only heard some of the conversation:

"If you don't mind me asking, I would like to know more about Anna." Kayato's voice said.

"It's been a month now since . . . . her parents have died" I heard my Grandpa say. "For a week she would just lie in bed, didn't go outside like she use to, wouldn't eat, only ate food when she wanted to, and would cry herself to sleep every night."

"You have to understand that she hasn't fully accepted that they're dead, but then again who does accepts death of someone they love who has passed away." Grandma said. I could hear the sadness in her voice.

"Then we decided we better do something, so we brought her Diego" Grandpa said. "Ever since then she has started to refocus on her training."

"Lisa was our daughter and David her husband, it was two weeks after their death, that we had a visit from King Jou and his wife Queen Rira, they wanted Anna to come and work for them as a night guard, she had already met their son Jai and his younger sister Mia. Anna and her parents met the South Royal Family about six months ago." That was the end of the conversation.

All the things I have put my grandparents through. As Diego came bounding towards me with the stick in his mouth he dropped it and I threw it again; he quickly got the stick and brought it back to me, he then dropped the stick halfway and kept running towards me.

"No Diego, don't you—" Too late he put his front paws on my thighs and pushed me down, I lightly fell on my back and kept my head up so I wouldn't hit it as I landed on the ground, Diego's pink tongue started licking my face.

"No Diego, stop that tickles." I laughed. I put up my hands and tried to stop Diego as I patted his head. But that didn't work. So I said in a stern voice "Diego stop."

He stopped and looked at me. "Good boy." I said as I got up from the ground.

He sat down. Then I heard footsteps, I looked out of the corner of my eye to see who it was, it was Kayato, I noticed he wore the white kimono it looked the same as the one he had on yesterday, but it had black on the collar. My Grandparents came down the steps as well.

"It's time to go now Anna." Kayato said.

"Okay, just a minute." I said.

He nodded and he walked over to his horse and got on, I walked over to my Grandparents and hugged them and said bye to them. I walked over to my horse and got on and set off for Kayato's place, Kayato caught up to me.

"Before, when we were at your Grandparent's house and were outside you were talking to me, how come you didn't say they had a dog?"

"You didn't ask." I replied with a smile.

It was after dinner, I was sitting on my bed when Dean stood in the door way.

"Anna, Kayato would like to speak to you." He said.

I stood up. "Okay, where is he?" I said a little nervous.

"He is on the back veranda."

As I started walking Dean asked "How are your Grandparents?"

"They're good." I answered him.

"Oh by the way Anna, Kayato doesn't like to be kept waiting." He said.

"Well then, why are we still here flapping our gums?" I smiled.

As I made my way out to the kitchen, Kayato was sitting outside just like Dean said he was; on the table was a bandage. I walked to the door frame. "Dean said you would like to speak to me."

"Yes Anna, please have a seat." He lightly said.

I walked to a chair and sat myself down.

"Last night Dean and I saw you talking to your friend May-Lyn." He said as he looked at me.

I looked down at the table and sighed.

"It's okay Anna, you're not in trouble. Dean was telling me about how you and May-Lyn found Snowbell." He said looking out at the garden.

"Yeah, that was a good day, did he tell you that we found her on the beach, so May-Lyn and me took care of her, we were both working for King Jou at the time, so we hid her away from him, but one day she was too fast for us and she found her way into the dining room where King Jou and his family were having lunch." I said.

"Yes" Kayato said. "And Dean also told me about King Jou and what had happened." Kayato said. "He told me about how the King's wife went away and hasn't been back since, and Dean said that King Jou told everyone who wants to speak to the South Royal Family, has to ask the King for permission first." He paused before continuing. "And that you were caught talking to Prince Jai, and the King found out and he had you arrested." He looked at me.

I just sat there and nodded. "And then I had to duel King Jou, I didn't want to . . . . but he wouldn't listen to me, I kept telling him no, and then his sword got me on my left arm, and that was that." As I said that I remembered the duel between me and King Jou.

"I saw your scar on your arm." Kayato said.

"When?" I said nervously.

"Last night, when you came back inside the house, you rubbed your sleeve and it revealed the scar." He said softly.

"Oh, that was what you were looking at." I said.

"Yes and I want to help you." He said calmly.

I put my left arm up on the table and pulled the sleeve of my kimono up to show the pink scar I didn't look at.

"Hold your arm out straight, please." Kayato told me.

As I held my arm out straight for him, I noticed my arm shaking, I tried very hard to keep it straight, as Kayato wrapped the bandage around my arm I decided to ask him a question while we were sitting, above us the lanterns were on.

"The head officer, that was here today, is he May-Lyn's father?" I asked him.

"Yes, King Daichi" Kayato said without taking his eyes off the bandage. "He takes good care of the villages in the

North" Kayato continued "That's where I met Yasumi; you see I use to work for King Daichi as a guard."

"And Yasumi, what did she do?" I asked him, wanting to know more.

"Yasumi worked as a cook for him and his wife way before they had May-Lyn." He replied.

He finished wrapping the bandage around my arm.

"Great, not only have a lied to an officer, but I lied to a king, May-Lyn told me that her father was an officer, I only have met him once." I said.

"King Daichi has a gift . . . . he can tell when people lie to him but he likes to find out why people have lied to him before he arrests them."

I just sat there in silence.

When Kayato started to speak again "Tell me a bit more about yourself." He said lightly.

"Well, my family moved from Australia to here when I was about four years old to the East region, you see my father's parents are from Australia but moved here when he was just a baby, and he came to Australia for a holiday, and that's where he met my mum, they met in 1990 and were married a year later, and then in 1992 I was born, and you probably know about my mother's parents are from Australia too." I said, he nodded.

"How long have you been friends with May-Lyn?" He asked me.

"We were both five, we met in the South village at a market, I kind of wandered off from my parents when they weren't looking, to look at a stall that was selling and making swords, May-Lyn was also there by herself too, and we watched the Blacksmith making the swords and she bumped into me. And said that she was sorry that she bumped into me, and she introduced herself to me and I also introduced myself to her, but when she introduced herself she didn't say Princess May-Lyn." I paused.

"Then what happened? Kayato asked.

"After we introduced ourselves to each other, I heard my parents calling my name, they were worried. At the same time somebody was calling May-Lyn's name, my parents and her parents got to shop at same time."

"And then?" Kayato's voice asked.

"When our parents finally got to shop, I ran straight to my mother and she picked me up and hugged me then put me down. Then my father knelt down and said in a stern voice "Anna, don't you ever do that again, you understand?" "I did understand and I never did it again" I said. "Then after a week that I had met May-Lyn, her father offered my father a job."

"And you had no idea that she was a Princess?" He asked.

"Nope no idea at all." I took another pause and started talking again "I'm also friends with May-Lyn's boyfriend Jiro, and my other friend Ema who lives in the East, where I spent most of my childhood, but up to six months ago we moved from there to live between the South and North regions, you see my Grandfather use to be a judge back in Australia and got offered a position here, so that's why he has a house guard." I said.

Kayato nodded.

"I apologise for the way I spoke to you earlier today, and that I took off to see my Grandparents without asking you, I was out of—" I tried to say.

"Anna, you don't have to apologise" He interrupted me. "And I'm certainly not going to punish you, that's not my job; my job is to train you." He said calmly. After Kayato and I had talked out on the veranda, I made my way to bed.

Chapter 3

It was now morning I rolled over so I was facing the door and stuck my left arm out from the cover, and moved my head, something licked my hand, as I turned my head to see what had licked my hand I could see a white bundle of fur, as I pulled my cover back and sat up to look, the white bundle of fur barked. *I know that bark.*

"Snowbell! What are you doing here?" I said.

I picked her up and made my way from my bedroom I snuck quietly out to the kitchen *creak* went a floor board. *Oops*, I checked the time it. *Good it's only 6:00 am.* I looked around to see if anybody was up. Nope nobody was up, which was good, I put Snowbell down, and she barked.

"Quiet Snowbell, you'll wakeup—" I was about to say.

"What's going on?"

I spun around to find Monikku standing behind me she wore a light yellow kimono. "You should be in bed." I said to her.

She rubbed her eyes and looked up at me. "I woke up early this morning." Her little voice said.

"Oh." I replied.

"This is Snow—" I tried to say.

"Snowbell." She interrupted me.

I looked at her. "You know her?" I asked.

"She jumped over the lowest part of the stone wall last night, Dad got such a shock when he saw a dog racing up towards him and Dean said it was Snowbell." She answered.

Just then Taro came out, he had muscle on him, and he only had shorts on. "Morning Monikku, morning Anna."

We both said good morning.

Monikku looked at Taro "Taro." She said as Taro walked towards the fridge.

"Yes?" He asked with his head poked in the fridge.

"Put a shirt on, we have a guest." She said. I smiled at what she had said.

"Maybe I'll put on a shirt, when you go back to bed; it's too early for you to be up." He answered.

As he got something from the fridge and turned around to face us Monikku poked her tongue out at him, and he poked his tongue at her, then walked up to the table and put his bottle of juice on the table and walked back to his bedroom. He came out with a black t-shirt on and smiled playfully at his little sister then walked to her.

"Taro, please don't." She said as she walked backwards. He took two quick steps towards her, picked her up and with his other hand started tickling her.

"Taro" She giggled "Please stop."

"Okay, okay I'll stop." He told her.

It was obvious that he respected his little sister. She reached round him to grab his bottle of juice, undid the lid and handed it Taro, he took it from her with his free hand and took a swig. He put it back down on the table and took the lid from Monikku and put it back on the bottle.

Emika then came out from her bedroom, she wore a purple kimono, she smiled at me and said morning, I said good morning to her.

"Hey babe." Taro said to her.

"Morning Taro." She said through a smile.

Taro then put Monikku down and she grabbed his hand.

"Come on, we better go to the stables to check on the horses."Taro said.

"Okay." She said with a smile still on her face.

She watched Taro and Monikku walk to the stables. We sat down at the kitchen table. "How long have you been going out with Taro?" I asked.

"Six months" She said happily. "We met each other while I was working at the local Inn, he was travelling to home from the West, and he kept coming back once a month, then that turned into once a week." She said "Then I finally asked him why he kept coming to the inn."

I smiled.

"He smiled and said to me that it wasn't because of the good service, it was because of the beautiful receptionist." She blushed as she said that.

"That's sweet." I said.

"The last time he came to the inn, he asked me out. But you're probably wondering why I stay here, with his family."

I nodded and said "Yes."

"My parent's work away, but they maintain a house nearby." She calmly said.

"Where do they work?" I asked.

"They work in the West; they come home twice a month and then go again." She answered my question.

"You must miss them a lot." I said sadly.

"Yeah I do." She said.

Just then, Taro and Monikku came up the back steps and came back into kitchen, Taro lent down and kissed Emika on the cheek, Dean walked into the kitchen and smiled, *I didn't hear him come in.*

"I'll be outside" I said to everyone who was in the kitchen "I want to meditate before breakfast."

As I walked down the wooden steps, I looked around the garden to find a nice place for mediation; I kept walking past the horse stables and saw another garden. It was absolutely beautiful; it had flowers around bricks that formed a love heart. *Wow! Now this is what I call a garden, should I meditate here? Is this still Kayato's property?* I thought, but before I could stop myself I sat down in a meditation position.

As I got up from my meditation position I walked slowly back to the house, I came closer to the side of the stone wall and saw Kayato and Yasumi sitting out on the back veranda, she had her hands placed ever so neatly on the table and he had his hand holding hers. I smiled to myself. *He cares for her a lot; I can tell that, they make a lovely couple.* I walked up the steps.

"Did you get a surprise this morning?" Kayato asked me.

"Yes I did, I wasn't expecting Snowbell to follow me here." I answered his question.

Yasumi smiled. "There's some breakfast still left, if it's not too late for you to have breakfast." She said.

Too late? What did she mean? I asked myself. "too late?" I asked her.

"It's 9:00 am." She assured me.

I looked at her. *What! Nine o'clock, already it can't be* I shouted in my head. "How long was I meditating for?" I asked in shock.

"Taro said you went out into garden about 6:15." Kayato answered me.

"Sorry" I said. "I'll make it up to you." I said to Kayato.

And then I quickly walked inside and got my breakfast and ate it. As I scoffed down the last bit of toast, I literally ran from the kitchen to my bedroom and grabbed any kimono I put my hands on. Ran down the hallway into the bathroom got changed, cleaned my teeth, put my night kimono on my bed and ran for the kitchen, I came to a halt when I realised that I didn't have my sword.

"Great!" I said to myself and quickly darted back down the hallway to my bedroom and grabbed my sword from its case.

I walked to the kitchen this time, and went outside to join Kayato, Dean . . . . And an elder! *An elder!* I was a little embarrassed because of what the elder would probably think of me for being late for this training session. Kayato smiled at me as I came down the steps once again, I smiled then I made it disappear. The elder wore a grey kimono I looked at him, and to my shock he wasn't smiling, I swear he didn't even blink when I looked at him, I must of blinked like twenty times while I was staring at him. *Is he even human?* He had black hair with some white showing, and was slightly shorter then Kayato.

"And now we begin." The elder said without warning.

"What begins now?" I asked the elder.

"Ask questions later girl!" The elder snapped at me.

Dean and Kayato were standing at my flanks; the elder drew his sword and rushed at me. *Three on one battle this was going to be easy* I thought. As I pulled my sword out and blocked his strike I went backwards and nearly fell. *Okay, no more mister nice guy, or should I say girl.* I thought to myself as I regained my balance. He pulled his sword into a downward strike, I barely blocked it.

"If this was a real battle, you would be shown no mercy!" The elder said to me.

I moved my sword and kicked at his wrist, he moved back and I went forward. Kayato then ran at the elder, they exchanged clashes of swords. When I ran at him, with my sword in upward strike he blocked it, Dean then came up from behind, somehow the elder knew that he was there, the elder moved to one side and Dean tumbled forward. *How did he know?* I thought to myself.

We were still standing after four hours of training I could barely move my left arm.

"Son." The elder said.

Son? I thought.

"Yes father." I heard Kayato's voice reply.

"Please introduce me to your student." The elder said.

"Anna, this is my father Kaishou." He said as he introduced his father to me.

"Nice to meet you, Anna." Kaishou said.

I shook hands with him.

"Pop!" I heard Monikku shout.

She ran at him, and he picked her up to hug her and then put her back down, still holding hands they walked inside together. Kayato smiled. Dean also went inside. Kayato and I sat at the round table that was on the back veranda.

"How's your arm?" Kayato asked me.

"I can barely move it." I answered him. He nodded.

"Did he make you train like that?" I asked him.

"Yes he did, but much harder." Kayato answered me.

"Oh." I said. "Sorry for being late this morning, the time just got away from me." I said.

"You're off the hook for being late from me." He assured me.

I thought of Jai, and what he would be doing. I sighed. The afternoon passed quickly and Kaishou went home.

My arm still ached, I suppose it was worth it, I smiled to myself; I sat down on my bed.

"Anna." Taro said, he stood in the door way.

"Hey Taro." I replied.

"Can I talk you?" He asked.

"Yes, you can Taro." I said to him.

"I'm thinking about asking Emika's hand in marriage, but I want to do it right, I want to ask her father for permission first" He paused "I guess she told you that her parent's work away and only come home twice a month." He said. I nodded.

"When do they come home again?" I asked him.

"They come home tomorrow." Taro said.

"And you want me to come with you?" I asked.

"If you don't mind." He said with a smile.

"Sure." I smiled. "Have you met her parents?" I asked.

"Yeah twice now." Taro answered my question.

Chapter 4

Bumping into an old friend

The next morning it turned out that everyone wanted to go to the market, Yasumi stayed behind because Monikku hadn't woken up yet and Emika was busy cooking. As Kayato, Taro, Dean and I made our way to the North markets, we parted into pairs; I went with Taro to see Emika's parents. Kayato and Dean went to the market. When Taro and I got to Emika's house, her parents were sitting in the garden. There was an arch and a beautiful garden. The house was wood, and painted light brown. When Taro and I approached Emika's parents both stood and greeted Taro. Taro introduced me to them.

"Anna, this is Mirai, Emika's father, and her mother Saika." Taro said.

"It's nice to meet you Anna." Mirai said.

"Same to you." I said with a smile.

I shook hands with him, and I noticed that he had a very strong hand. Then I shook hands with Saika.

"Welcome Anna" Saika said. "Please have a seat." She had beautiful brown eyes.

"Thank you." I said with a smile.

"How is Emika?" Mirai said.

Taro answered with a smile. "She's good, she's cooking today."

Taro told me how Emika took him to meet her parents, he fell up the step. I imagined Taro when he fell up the step. I guessed he must have been nervous. After Taro told me the story he asked Mirai if they could speak in private. They got up and walked to the big cherry tree that was on the right hand side of the house.

"How long have you been staying with Kayato's family?" Saika asked me.

"Four days so far." I answered with a smile, she smiled back at me.

I heard Taro talking to Emika's father:

"I love your daughter so much, and I come here today to ask you permission to ask for her hand in marriage."Taro said to Emika's father, I could her that he was nervous when he spoke.

"You are willing to take care of her?" Emika's father asked Taro.

"Yes sir." Taro said.

"And you are going to love her no matter what?" He asked.

"Yes." Taro answered him.

"Well then welcome to the family." He said.

As they walked over to the table where Emika's mother and I were sitting Taro and Mirai sat back down.

After we had morning tea with them, Taro and I said bye, and headed back to the North markets where Kayato and Dean were. We found Kayato and Dean having morning tea. We took a seat at the table.

"Would you like some morning tea?" Kayato asked us as we sat down.

"No thanks." I answered him.

"Taro?" He asked his son.

"Yes please." Taro said.

"Taro we have already—" I started to say.

Taro looked at me, and put his finger up to his lips as if he was telling me to be quiet. *How much can he eat?* As they ate and sipped their tea I thought of *Prince Jai again, and wondered if Kayato's father had visited him also.* Then a voice snapped me back to reality.

"Anna!" A voice said.

As I turned in my chair to see who it was, I got up and went to greet him. He was standing near the fence where our horses were.

"Akashi!" I shouted out as I made my way to him.

He hugged me as I got closer to him. His brown kimono stuck out against his skin.

"Hey." He said after he let go of me.

"Hey." I said after I could breathe again. His black hair had gotten longer since the last time I saw him, which was a year ago.

"What are you doing here?" He asked, his brown eyes sparkled in the sun

"On business." I answered him "So how is everything?"

"Yeah, same as usual." He answered with a smile.

I was about to ask him a question when I noticed someone behind Akashi. Akashi noticed my distraction and turned round to see what I was looking at. *Oh no* I shouted in my head. It was Akashi's father who was standing just a couple feet away from us.

"I'd better get back to work; I guess I'll see you around sometime." Akashi said.

I began walking away from Akashi's father and I noticed that Kayato, Dean and Taro were standing up not very far away from us.

"Anna!" Araki shouted behind me.

I stopped and turned around. "What?" I asked him.

"What are you doing here?" He asked rudely.

"I'm here on business." I answered.

"You shouldn't be here!" He almost yelled at me.

"You still blame me for what happened to Akashi, don't you?" I asked him.

"What do you think?" He said. "What happened to Akashi was an accident." I said, as I turned and walked away.

"You love him!" Akashi's father yelled.

I turned around once again. "Yes, I do love him." I snapped at him.

He walked away and I walked over to the fence where the horses were.

I then said to Dean and Kayato. "Let's get out of here." We rode off back to Kayato's place.

Night had fallen and I was out on the back veranda, I was leaning my arms on the rail of the veranda when Kayato and Dean came out, Kayato asked me about the confrontation between Araki and me.

"Twelve months ago Akashi and I were coming back from the west from delivering freight. I was ahead of Akashi when his horse got spooked by some people. He fell and broke his back. When Akashi got home he stayed in bed, I wasn't allowed to see him, but I snuck into his room sometimes when his father wasn't there, just to see how he was. But one day I wasn't quick enough getting out of his room and his father caught me trying to sneak out of Akashi's bedroom window. And so he yelled at me, he told me to never come back there. So I haven't been back, not since today." I said sadly.

"And so I went to live with my grandparents, but before I left Akashi's I left him a letter. I made another copy of the letter; I carry it with me everywhere." I took it out from my kimono sleeve and handed it to Kayato and he started reading it:

Dear Akashi,
I am so sorry what had happened to you. I'm not coming back; I just hope you can forgive me for all of this . . . . you just concentrate on getting better. I'm going to live with my Grandparents for a while, I don't want you to come and visit me there at all, not even when you get better.
~~Love,~~
From Anna.

"His father still blames me for what happened to Akashi."
I said sadly.

"But, Anna it wasn't your fault." Kayato said softly.

"I know" I said quietly. "If you don't mind I'll just spend
sometime in the garden."

"Please take your time." Kayato said.

They went inside; I didn't worry about getting the letter
back. I decided to meditate near the stone wall. I sat down
and got comfortable, *I once again thought about Prince Jai,
and what had happened today. I flashed back to when I was
first staying with the Prince and his family. One day Prince Jai
and his sister Princess Mia and I were sitting down outside and
they were talking and having fun.*

There was a noise. *What now?* I got up and started walking;
I withdrew my sword as quietly as I could, and kept
walking.

"Anna!" Prince Jai's voice whispered.

I looked toward the stone wall. And put my sword back.
"Jai!" I said. "You shouldn't be here."

"I so should be here you are very important to me." He
said.

I blushed and kneeled to my Prince.

"Don't kneel, you are creeping me out." He said.

"Sorry. Kayato has taught me well." I said.

"Oh I've missed you." He said as he came up to me until the wall stopped him.

I playfully pushed him. He wrapped his arms around me like a big bear hug, I smiled, and I had my eyes closed I then opened them and looked up and saw Dean staring at me.

"Anna?" He said wide eyed "What are you doing?" He asked me.

I was confused. I tried to speak but I couldn't. I felt Jai's arms unwrap, he was still on the other side of the wall, so what harm could this be doing? We weren't doing anything wrong, we were just hugging, and well he was hugging me.

"Nothing." Jai answered him.

Dean just stared at Jai. *Right this is awkward. What am I going to do?* I thought to myself.

"Would you like to come inside?" I asked the Prince.

"Yes, I would like that." The Prince said.

I moved back from the wall and Jai put one hand on the wall and pushed, he landed on the other side.

"I'll tell Kayato we have company." Dean said and headed back to the house.

I smiled and started to walk back to the house also, Jai put his hand in mine. I looked at our hands and smiled, he lightly swung our hands back and forth.

As we sat down at the table I noticed that Monikku was looking at Jai, her little brown eyes wide. Just then Kayato made a coughing sound. Monikku looked at her father, and he looked at her and then she started eating her dinner. I smiled to myself and started to eat my dinner.

After dinner Taro lightly took Emika by the hand and led her outside. *Yes! He is going to propose to her I* thought, and that also brought a smile to my face.

Kayato helped with the washing up, and Monikku went off, I guess to her bedroom, so it was only Jai, Dean and I left at the table. Jai took my hand again and we stood up, and went outside. He smiled and squeezed my hand. I wanted to tell him that I loved him, well I think I did.

"What are you thinking about?" He asked.

"My parents." I answered him sadly. He hugged me. *I don't want him to let go.*

"Yes!" Taro shouted.

I looked over at the far garden and Taro hugged Emika and then he picked her up and slowly spun around and then put her back on the ground. Another smile came to my face, Taro *and Emika are engaged I* said to myself. Just then Jai unwrapped his arms from around me.

"Thank you for inviting into Kayato's house." He said with a smile.

"That's okay." I replied.

He leaned in to my face. *My first kiss!*

"I'd better go." He suddenly said.

He moved his head and lightly kissed my right cheek. He was down the steps before I could say bye and I watched him as he jogged over to the stone wall and leapt over it. "Bye Jai." I said with a sigh.

I made my way back into the kitchen "Was that Taro we heard shout?" Yasumi asked.

I smiled and nodded. "He just asked Emika to marry him." I answered her.

Great me and my big mouth. Taro would want them to know, but he would have liked to tell them himself with Emika.

"But hey, don't say that I told you, just act surprise okay." I said a moment later.

I could have kicked myself for saying that Taro proposed to Emika. I made my way to my bedroom grabbed my night kimono and headed for the bathroom. I quickly brushed my teeth, and had a quick shower and slowly made my way back to my bedroom. Out in the kitchen Taro and Emika had announced that they were engaged. Even though I have been staying here for four days, and got to know them, I was happy for them.

I was under the cover, when I started to remember that horrible day; May-Lyn and I were out in the ocean, we were swimming and having fun, when all of a sudden my ankle got stuck, I was going under, and May-Lyn saved me. *I owe May-Lyn a lot* I told myself.

Just then Monikku came into my bedroom, she was crying. "Anna." She said.

I sat up, but didn't take the cover off. "Hey sweetie, what's the matter?" I asked her.

She looked at me with her brown eyes and then she burst out into tears. She walked up to the bed and climbed on I hugged her.

"I-I didn't mean to break it." She said in a nervous voice.

"Break what?" I asked her.

"This" She said, she opened her little hand, and on her palm was a broken piece of glass. "Mummy brought it for Daddy, it was his birthday present." She informed me.

"What was it before you accidently broke it?" I asked. It was thick glass, by the looks of it; it was a glass animal ornament.

"It was in a shape of a duck; well it was until I broke it." She answered me.

"Tell me what happened." I said softly.

"Well I was in the lounge and I got up to go to bed and I went to grab my drink of water from the coffee table and the glass duck was near the edge, when I accidently bumped it and fell and broke." She answered my question.

"Where was your Dad when this happened?" I asked her.

"He was outside." She said.

"You have to tell him what happened." I said softly.

Monikku shook her little head. "No, I don't want to tell him." She said.

"How about I go with you?" I asked.

"Okay." She said.

So I got up from my bed, Monikku stood up, and we both walked down the hallway to the kitchen and Monikku stopped.

"Oh look at that he's busy. Goodnight Anna." She said, and pulled me back down the hallway.

"Monikku you have to tell him" I said. "It's not going to be all bad." I assured her.

She once again shook her head, "Can't you just tell him that you broke it?" She asked.

"That would be lying; telling a lie only makes things more difficult." I answered her.

"Okay, I'll guess I'll tell him." She said.

"Just tell him exactly what you told me, and you'll be fine." I said.

As we walked to the kitchen, Monikku stopped and hid behind me. "Kayato." I said.

"Yes Anna." He said without taking his eyes of what he was reading.

"Monikku would like talk to you." I said.

Just then Monikku's arm grabbed my leg. "Monikku." Her father said looking at us.

But she still had hold of my leg, I started to walk to Kayato with her grabbing my leg, but that didn't work.

"Monikku." Her father said again.

I noticed her peeping out from behind my leg. She then let go of my leg, and ran at the table, she put the broken piece of glass on the table.

"Here Dad, sorry I didn't mean to break it." She said then turned to run off again.

But before she could Kayato grabbed her by her hand and pulled her onto his lap, she sat there looking at me. I wasn't sure what I suppose to do at this point. I nodded at her.

And then I turned to leave the kitchen and go back and lie down. "Anna." Kayato said.

Now I was the one who was nervous. "Yes Kayato." I managed to say.

"Please have a seat." He said calmly.

I turned around and made my way over to a seat and sat down. *Um what now?* I asked myself. Monikku had her little back resting against her father's stomach and chest and was looking at the broken piece of glass.

"What happened?" Kayato asked his daughter.

"It was an accident Daddy" She said, her voice still nervous. "I got up to go to bed and I grabbed my drink of water when I accidently bumped the glass duck and it fell and broke." She said with tears in her eyes.

Kayato just sat there in silence for a moment. "Thank you for telling me." Kayato said to his daughter.

Monikku burst out crying again. He hugged his daughter.

"Calm down." He said softly to her.

Monikku calmed down a bit, he stroked her hair lightly.

"You did the right thing, by telling me what happened, Monikku." He said.

This made her smile. She climbed off his lap and said goodnight to us. We both said goodnight to her, and she rushed for her bedroom.

"I'll be in soon to tuck you in." Kayato shouted.

"Okay." Monikku shouted back.

This made me smile. I then too said goodnight to Kayato and made my way back to my bedroom. I noticed that on my bedside table was the letter that I had handed to Kayato for him to read. I didn't notice it there before.

That night I dreamed of Akashi and me, and how we bumped into each other at the North market, but in the dream May-Lyn was there, I was talking to her and all of the village people were looking at me like I had gone bonkers, it was like I was the only one that could see her in my dream. She was saying something to me, but I couldn't hear her. I woke up, I looked at the clock it was only 5:00 am. I looked down to see if Snowbell was still sleeping. *Good* I thought. I decided to go and meditate; I grabbed my red kimono and headed for the bathroom. Once out of the bathroom, I checked on Snowbell and chucked my night kimono on my pillow and wandered to the kitchen and creak went the floor board. *Not again!* I told myself. I quietly opened the door and walked out onto the veranda, as I made my way to the garden *Jai, Jai, Jai, Jai* I kept telling myself or was it my heart? I sat down and started to meditate, I thought of last night and how Jai visited me, and then I thought we were going to share our first kiss. Damn it, why didn't I just kiss him! But would it be wrong of me to do so? I opened my eyes and started to cry. And made my way back to the house I ran from the kitchen to my bedroom, jumped in bed and stayed there. *Am I falling in love with Prince Jai??* I asked myself over and over again. It was now the fifth day I was staying with Kayato and his family. And in those five days I have already learnt so much about myself and my training.

Chapter 5

Confused

It was now 7:00 am, I decided to get up and have some breakfast, and I didn't eat much. I didn't feel like eating at all but I had to. I figured today I was going to be training none stop because we missed a training session yesterday. Taro and Emika had gone to her parent's house to spend the day with them; they had to go back to work tomorrow. As I sat there quietly eating my breakfast Jai's name kept popping up in my head. *Am I obsessed with the Prince, or what!*

After we ate, we went straight into training; I wasn't really focusing on what we were doing. I was still thinking about Prince Jai. Kayato rushed at me, he had his sword into a downward strike, I barley blocked it. *Focus!* I told myself. Kayato stopped what he was doing and looked at me.

"Anna?" He said. I just stood there, I didn't answer him.

"Anna?" It was Dean who said my name for the second time.

"What?!" I suddenly snapped at Dean.

Dean just stood there looking at me. Kayato put his sword away and sat down. "Focus." Dean said.

I looked at him, *Easy for you to say, you're parents are not dead, and I'm confused about Prince Jai* I told myself and I wanted to say it so badly to him, but I thought that I better not. I looked to where Kayato was sitting down.

"I'm ready now." I said to him.

He got up, and took out his sword and rushed at me, I heard Dean take out his sword from behind me, and I blocked Kayato's strike and then moved to my left and turned and blocked Dean's strike. We trained two against one for nearly most of the day. I was tired after we had lunch, but I kept it up to see how long I could last. It was five o'clock in the afternoon when we finally finished. *Wow! That was the longest training session I have ever had.* I was proud of myself. As we made our way to the table Jai's name popped up in my head again.

At dinner I mostly thought of Prince Jai and wondered what he would be having for dinner. I missed his smile most of all; the way he respected people, his kindness, his generosity to helping people. I quickly ate my dinner, rushed to my bedroom I put my sword back in its case and took off my locket and put it down on the bedside table to where the letter still was, grabbed my night kimono and headed to the bathroom, after I cleaned my teeth and had a shower I walked slowly back to my bedroom. I sat down on my bed, and decided to get my photo album. I grabbed it from my luggage and flipped through it until I came to a photo of Jai and me. He had his red and gold kimono on and I wore my pink kimono, we were at the front of the palace when the photo was taken. He secretly had a hold of my hand, and next to the photo there was another photo in this photo he had his arm around my lower back. *I think I love Prince Jai!* I told myself. I quickly shut the photo album and it went thump! I put it back in my luggage where it belonged. Snowbell came into my bedroom. I picked her up and held her close to my chest.

"What am I going to do?" I said to her, she licked my cheek; I patted her and put her in her bed.

I pulled back the cover of my bed and lay there, then I got up again to turn off the light, I stumbled about making my way to bed. I got in bed and pulled the cover up; my hand ached from holding my sword for most of the day. But it was worth it. I thought of Prince Jai as I lied in bed, I felt a tear run down my cheek and I started to cry lightly.

I rolled over, wiping the tears away from my eyes. *What was wrong with me?* How am I going to explain to Kayato what happened in training today when he asks me when I don't even know myself? I guess I could tell him that I wasn't focused but then he probably just make me train even harder, or might yell at me and tell me to start focusing. Maybe I should do less meditating and start training even harder then today. As I lie in bed thinking up some excuse to tell Kayato if he does ask me what happened today in training, I thought of May-Lyn and Jiro hoping their okay and then I remembered what King Daichi had told me when I asked what would happen to her if she gets caught: *She might be put in the North castle jail.* King Daichi words echoed in my head. *How long will she be in jail? She is the*

Princess of the North, so the guards will have to listen to her, won't they? I thought as I drifted off to sleep.

It was early next morning when I woke up, I grabbed my purple kimono and headed off to the bathroom, I made my way back to my bedroom and on my way back I grabbed my sword and folded my night kimono and neatly placed it on my bed. Jai's name came in my head again. I grabbed a pen and some pieces of paper from my luggage and went out to the kitchen, nobody was up and I walked around the creaky floor board and sat down at the table and started writing.

To Prince Jai,
How are you?

That wouldn't sound right to him; he's use to being called Your Highness or Prince Jai or Your Royal Highness Prince Jai

I got new piece of paper and started again.

To the Prince,
I'm glad you visited me the other night; I had fun and enjoyed your company. I miss you, I have been thinking about you a lot lately.
From Anna.

That's all I could think of, should I ride over to the palace and sneak in and leave it on his bedside table? But if I get caught I will be arrested. *Oh well* I thought as I got up from the table grabbed the letter and folded it neatly and put it in the sleeve of my kimono. I put my writing kit away back in my luggage. I walked quickly to the stables and saddled my horse then headed south. As I passed the wooden bridge I knew I was just outside the palace walls, I got off my horse and walked him over to a tree and tied his reigns loosely around a branch, just in case I needed to get away fast. I walked to the edge of the white wall and peered around the corner to see if there were guards. There were two of them dressed in maroon, which was the official colour of the South Officers.

Great, that's all I need I said to myself, I pulled my head back and looked at the ground there were some small stones on the ground, I picked up a handful of them, I picked out two and put them in my left hand and put the rest in my right hand, and then I poked my head around the corner again I quickly threw the handful of stones into some bushes which were on the right of me and quickly pulled my head back. I heard one of the guards say:

"What was that?"

"We better go and have a look." The other guard said with a sigh.

After they went to check, I ran as fast as my legs would let me, I quietly opened the palace doors, and headed for Prince Jai's bedroom. As I made my way along the first hallway there was another guard. *I should have got more stones.* I lightly took a step back around the corner and threw the stone. The guard went to see what was going on. I went along another hallway I quickly but silently walked along the hallway to Prince Jai's room. I stopped as I came to the golden door, I sighed. And I quietly opened the door, the room was fairly big.

"Wow." I said out aloud. Then I quickly put my hand over my mouth. *Shut it. I don't want to get caught again. Especially in the Prince's bedroom.* Prince Jai was still asleep; he looked so handsome when he was sleeping. His bed was king sized and had those curtains on the side. And then I looked over to his wardrobe it was huge. I walked over to his bedside table and placed the letter down. I quickly walked back to his bedroom door, opened it and made my way out into the hallway. As I came back to the first hallway the guard still wasn't back, so I made my way to the front door quietly opened it, the guards who were guarding the palace door weren't back either. I took a quick look around to see if I could see them, nope no sign of them, but I still ran from the palace door to the wall. I still had the stone in my hand; I dropped it and made my back to my horse. I untied his reigns got on and headed back to Kayato's house.

When I got back to Kayato's house I went straight to the stables, unsaddled my horse, and gave him a wash and brushed him.

"At least you don't blame me for what happened to Akashi." I said to him as I patted his blazer. I talked to him as if he could understand me.

He had some hay still left over, and he started munching on that. I made my way back to the house, I quickly walked into the kitchen and checked the time, it was 7:00 am and nobody was up so I made my way back to bed.

I flashed back to when May-Lyn and I had the conversation when I finally woke up when she saved my life from nearly drowning. May-Lyn was standing in the door way. She looked at me and a smile came to her face. And the conversation we had:

"Good to see you're okay." She said.

"What happened?" I asked dazed.

"Remember, you and I were swimming in the ocean, and your foot got caught up in seaweed and you were going under and I saved you." She answered.

"Thank you."

"It's okay; I know you would do the same for me."

Then talking from the kitchen snapped me back to reality, got up slowly, I didn't want to get up out of the comfy bed I wanted to stay in bed all day. I walked to the door way and slowly but surely made my way into the kitchen. Once again Prince Jai's name came into my head and also Akashi's name. I quietly made my way to a seat and sat down. Monikku looked at me with her brown eyes. I ate breakfast and washed up.

"You don't have to do that." Yasumi's soft voice said.

"It's okay, I want to." I said as I turned to face her. She nodded, I noticed that she was holding Kayato's hand or was he holding hers? I couldn't tell. I finished washing up Kayato stood up, gee he's quick.

"After you Anna." Kayato said as he gestured towards the door.

I walked outside Kayato followed; I noticed that Dean didn't follow. *Great, now I wished that I stayed in be*d. I walked down the steps and walked a bit and then stopped and turned to face Kayato. He just looked at me and I looked at him.

"What happened yesterday?" He asked.

Um, um that's it I had no idea what I was going to tell him. I just kept looking at him thinking what to say.

"I had my mind somewhere else." I finally answered him a bit nervously.

"Don't you know what could of happened if that was a real duel!" He snapped at me.

"Yes, and I'm sorry it won't happen again." I said.

Then he walked off back into the house. *Okay, uh what now? Was training off for today? Ugh I was so confused.* I walked over to the stone wall and sat down. *Anna focus! Just stop thinking about the Prince all of the time* I told myself. Just then Dean came out to the garden. *Great, what does he want?*

"Kayato told me to tell you that training is off for today."

"I figured that when he went back into the house." I said.

"Anna please—" He started to say.

"What?!" I snapped at him.

He looked at me wide eyed. "What's with you lately, this isn't like you, not to be focusing" He said calmly. "Kayato is trying to help you."

I stood up. "Help me! Well excuse me; I didn't ask for any help, you got that!" I said. "You have no idea what's with me, you have no idea what I have gone through in the last month, and with Akashi. Sorry that I don't seemed focus, because I will not focus when I'm like this."

"Obvious." Dean muttered under his breath.

I glared at him. Then I walked back to the house, and out on the front veranda and kept walking north. I kept walking until some hours later I reached the North markets. Pass the market, I saw the North palace. Then I focused on a stall selling swords. *Maybe I should buy one, to make up for today.* I thought. I decided not to buy one and kept looking around the markets.

Then I recognised someone in the market, Kaishou and there was a woman with him holding hands. He looked straight at me. *Uh oh, what's he going to say when finds out that Kayato isn't here.* I kept walking pretending not see them, but it was hard not to look in their direction.

"Anna." Kaishou called out to me.

"Hey Kaishou." I replied.

The woman that was with him smiled. "This is my wife Tamaki." Kaishou introduced me to his wife.

"Nice to meet you Anna." She said with a smile.

"It's nice to meet you too." I said through a smile.

"Is Kayato here?" Kaishou asked me.

"Uh, he's around here somewhere." I lied, but then again it might be true, he might be looking for me.

He looked at me and smiled. *Has he have the gift to tell when people lie too?*

"Anna." Said another male voice.

I turned to see who it was. Thank goodness it was only Akashi. He walked over to me with a smile. I smiled back. He nudged me.

"Kaishou, Tamaki this is my friend Akashi." I introduced them to Akashi.

"Hello." Kaishou said.

"Nice to meet you." Tamaki said.

"Nice to meet you both." Akashi said with a smile.

"We don't mean to rush off, but we better get going." Kaishou said.

I nodded. "It was nice meeting you Tamaki."

"You too, and you Akashi." She said.

They walked off still holding hands; I looked past them and saw Kayato. *Uh oh.* I grabbed Akashi's wrist and pulled him and myself behind a market stall. Akashi looked at me. "What's wrong?" He asked.

"I shouldn't be here."

"Huh?" He looked confused.

"Yesterday I wasn't focusing on training and this morning Kayato kind of went off at me, and then I got into an argument with Dean. And then I walked off and decided to visit the North markets."

"Oh."

I looked at the ground and kicked at a small stone. I didn't know what to do now. Akashi grabbed my wrist and lightly pulled me over to another market stall.

"If you don't mind me asking, why weren't you focusing?" He asked lightly.

"I was," I paused "thinking about Prince Jai."

Akashi looked at me and smiled. After we spent some time at markets we went back to his house.

"Is your father home?" I asked a bit nervous.

"No he's at work."

Thank goodness I thought to myself. He opened the front door for me; we walked into the kitchen and sat down at the table. *I bet Kayato seen his father and asked if he had seen me. I bet he is so mad at me for what happened yesterday and this morning.*

"I saw your Grandparents yesterday." Akashi informed me.

"You did, how were they?" I asked through a smile.

"Their good, they wanted to know if you had seen me yet, and I told them about how I bumped into you."

"Yeah."

"Kaishou is an elder?" Akashi asked.

"Yes. The woman that was with him is his wife. They are Kayato's parents." I answered him.

Akashi nodded. We sat there in silence for a bit.

"Did you enjoy the markets?" Akashi piped up.

"Yeah I did, and it was nice bumping into you again." I said with a smile.

He smiled and showed his white teeth. Just then Akashi looked at me. "You better go; my father will be home soon." He warned me.

"Okay." I said.

I got up and Akashi stood up as well, he walked me to his door and hugged me then opened the door and he quickly shut it.

"Akashi, what's the matter?" I asked concerned.

"Let's go to the back door." He said as he lightly grabbed my hand. He walked past the kitchen into the lounge then Akashi led me down a hallway pass the bathroom and past some bedrooms and down a small hallway and there was the back door. He let go of my hand and hugged me again. As he opened the door I quickly walked out and looked back at Akashi, he put his hand up as if to wave bye but then he shut the door. *Okay, that was kind of weird. Should I go back to Kayato's or stay around the markets a bit more? I had no idea what to do, once again I was confused.*

I decided it would be best if I went back to Kayato's. As I started to walk from the back of Akashi's I turned my head to the right and saw Araki standing a few feet away.

"Back again, Anna." Araki said.

It wasn't a question. "Yes, I just wanted to see how Akashi was" I answered. "I better get going."

I started walking away from him but I didn't get very far. "Kayato is looking for you." He informed me.

"I bet he is." I sighed.

Then I started heading towards the North markets, as I walked along the dirt path there were trees on both sides, it wasn't a long walk from Akashi's to the markets. Then I saw Kayato at a market stall. *Um, um should I go and approach him now or take this opportunity and head back to his place?* I quickly walked past the market stall he was at and kept walking until I got out of the market. *That was close!* I then walked back to Kayato's deciding what I should do. It was a long walk from the North markets to Kayato's. As I finally got back to Kayato's I went straight out into the garden and got into a meditating position. *I seem to do better in my training sessions when I meditate before we start training but I can't seem to get Prince Jai's name out of my head.* I meditated for a while and then I got interrupted by footsteps. I stood up quietly and waited.

"Anna." It was a female voice this time. I knew the voice.

I turned my head to the right to see who it was. "May-Lyn." I managed to say as I walked over to the stone wall. *I was confused once again. What was she doing here?*

She was dressed in a light blue kimono. I stopped a few feet away from the wall and she leapt over the wall once again, but Jiro wasn't with her this time.

"What?" I started to say.

She looked at me and smiled. "What's what?" She said.

What the hell is wrong with me! I wanted to say to her. I wanted to tell her so much, but yet there wasn't enough time to tell it in.

69

"Is everything okay?" I finally said.

"Uh, that depends" She answered. "Is everything okay here? I mean with Kayato and Dean?"

Okay, this is getting too weird, first of all she takes off to the East, and then a couple of days later I have an argument with Kayato and Dean. And then she turns up here and asks me if everything is okay with them.

"Yep, everything is fine." I lied to her.

"Are you sure?"

"Yes, everything is good." I lied again and forced a smile on my face.

I felt sick at this point, I wonder what the punishment was if you lied to a Princess who is your best friend.

I sat down on the stone wall and rested my back against it, May-Lyn sat beside me. We didn't say anything for a while we just there in silence.

"Is anyone else home or is it just you?" She asked.

"I wouldn't have a clue; I have been out for most of the day."

"Okay." She said with a cheeky smile on her face.

"May, what are you thinking of?" Before she could answer my question, she got up and started walking towards to back veranda.

"May-Lyn, where are you going?" I called out to her.

She didn't answer me, but looked behind her and looked at me, she still had the cheeky smile on her face. I got up and walked after her. I caught up to her and she stopped at the foot of the wooden steps, I nearly bumped into her I was that close behind her.

"May—" I started say.

She looked at me and put her finger to her lips. "Hear that?" She said.

"No I don't hear anything." I answered her.

"Well then, nobody's home so it's safe for me to be here."

My mouth nearly dropped open when she said that. What did she mean by "Well then, nobody's home so it's safe for me to be here?" What? So if somebody else was home it wouldn't be safe for her to visit me? Was her father still looking for her? I had so many questions to ask her, I wouldn't worry about telling her about me.

She walked up the wooden steps and stopped. "Maybe I shouldn't do this." She said.

"Huh?" I asked.

"Shouldn't be on the back veranda, just in case someone does come home, I'll go back to sitting on the stone wall." She said as she made her way down the steps. I followed her and sat down next to her.

"So May-Lyn or should I say Princess May-Lyn?" I asked. She looked at me with shock. "About that" She said. "I was going to tell you that I am a Princess but—" She stopped.

I looked at her, and she looked at the ground.

"May-Lyn?" I asked. It wasn't like her to stop saying a sentence half way through. She looked at me

"I was going to tell you that I am a Princess, when we were both at your grandparents house and it was raining, but then Dean arrived to tell you . . . . that your parents had died from being ambushed, and since then I haven't found the right time to tell you, sorry." She said.

"You have nothing to be sorry about" I assured her. "I have a lot to be to be sorry for."

She looked at me with a shocked face. We sat in silence for a bit. Well it was true; I did have a lot to be sorry for. She looked at the veranda; I followed at what she was looking at. I wanted to go away and hide somewhere. Kayato was on the back veranda and looking straight at us.

"May you better go." I warned her. I didn't want her to get in trouble. She got up and I stood up as well.

"Bye Anna." She said.

And she quickly walked towards the stone wall and leapt over it. I didn't know what to do now so I just stood there. *This is absolutely great isn't it? Too bad this wasn't a nightmare and I could wake up, but no it wasn't a nightmare. This was reality.* And I had to face Kayato soon and I bet he's not going to let me get away with it this time. I sighed and sat down I looked at the ground only for a second and when I looked at the veranda Kayato wasn't there. *Right*; I got up and quickly walked into the house. He wasn't in the kitchen; he wasn't in the lounge room. There was nobody here but me, it was like Kayato wasn't even at the back veranda. I looked at the clock in the kitchen it was 4:00 pm in the afternoon, I decided to go back to the garden and meditate. I opened my eyes from my meditation, it was dark I got up and walked back to the house, it was in darkness except for where the lanterns were. *What was the time?* I stopped and waited for about forty-five minutes for my night vision to work. I then started to make my way up to the house and up the steps carefully. I opened the door and stepped into the kitchen and tried looking at the clock to see what time it was. I couldn't really see it properly it looked like the time was 10:45 pm. I made my way to the lounge room and carefully down the hallway until I came to my bedroom, I turned on my bedroom light.

"Uh that's bright!" I said.

I grabbed my night kimono and shut my bedroom door on my way out so it wouldn't wake up Dean. I quickly had a shower and cleaned my teeth and rushed back to my bedroom turned off the light and made my way to bed. I thought of Prince Jai once again.

Next morning I woke up grabbed my yellow kimono and headed to the bathroom. As I past my bedroom I placed my kimono on my bed and kept walking towards the kitchen. Taro and Emika were sitting at the table.

"Morning." Taro and Emika said at the same time.

"Good morning." I said a bit a nervous.

As I was about to put the spoonful of cereal in my mouth I nearly dropped it when Taro moved his hand off of Emika's hand. Her left hand had the most beautiful diamond ring, the diamond was huge! I quickly shoved the spoonful of cereal in my mouth so it didn't look like I was sitting there with my mouth hanging open. *Wow that must have cost Taro fair bit.* I slowly ate my breakfast; Taro, Emika and I were the only ones in the kitchen.

"Where is everybody?" I asked confused.

"Dad and Dean are outside waiting for you. And Mum and Monikku are at the market." Taro said happily.

"Oh . . . okay." I answered.

I finished off my breakfast and washed up, then made my way to my bedroom, grabbed my sword and then went to the bathroom to clean my teeth. I didn't want to go outside; I didn't even want to train today. I made my way back into the kitchen where Taro and Emika were still sitting. I looked at the clock it was 8:30 am. I opened the door and walked down the steps. *I could run to the stables and saddle my horse and just take off, but then Kayato will probably find me, he always does.* I stopped when I got down the last step. *Where are they? They are probably out the front. Oh well I'm not going out there, if they want me to train they have to come here.*

Just then I heard voices, they were coming from the stables. I made my way to the stables and saw Kayato talking to Dean; I stopped several feet away from them. Kayato was the first one to notice that I was there. He looked at me but this time without a smile. *Oh that's just great now he's mad at me.* I took a step back he just kept looking at me, and then I notice Dean walking up towards me. I wanted to run away but I just stood there. *Stay calm* I told myself. When Dean finally reached me he grabbed my wrist and pulled me back towards the stone wall. He stopped and let go of my wrist when I couldn't see Kayato anymore.

"What are you doing?" He asked me.

"Excuse me?" I asked shocked. "Why did you just pull me away like that?"

I said as he started to walk away from me. He spun around. "Because Anna it's none of your concern." He said rudely. And then he kept walking.

"Dean, what's the matter?" I asked.

He didn't answer me; he just kept walking back to the stables. *Excuse me, hello what am I suppose to do? Just sit here and twiddle my thumbs am I? Right this was getting too weird, I don't like this at all.* I walked back inside into the kitchen.

"Anna, what happened?" Taro asked.

"Nothing happened." I answered him as I walked to my bedroom.

I sat down on my bed and thought about Jai and what he would be doing. I looked to see if Snowbell was in her bed, she wasn't. She must be with Yasumi and Monikku. *I could go out the front and train, well just practice the upward strikes and downward strike and stuff like that.* I got up and walked to the lounge and down the hallway and opened the door and stepped out on the front veranda and walked down the steps onto the grass. I noticed that the guards weren't at the front door. Today must be their day off considering today was Saturday, that was nice of Kayato giving them the weekend off.

I pulled out my sword and did a downward strike and then an upward strike. Then I repositioned the sword so it was just above my waist and pulled it forward then back, I then did a forward flip and pointed the sword straight in front of me and then took a side step and pulled the sword back. I trained by myself until lunch time.

After lunch Kayato and I went back outside. *He probably is going to yell at me again, oh well I guess I deserve it.* He walked down the steps and walked a bit further and then came to a sudden stop. If I wasn't watching I would have ran into him. He turned around to face me and opened his mouth to speak. *And the yelling session begins* I thought.

"When I yelled at you yesterday I didn't mean to. I'm not normally like that." Kayato said calmly.

"It's okay" I said. "But what was with Dean this morning?"

"I brought Taro and Emika a house, they don't know yet. They can move in once they are married. If they would like to."

"You and Dean were talking about that?" I asked "Dean could have just told me, instead of—" I stopped myself.

Kayato looked at me.

"I guess Dean told you about the argument we got into?" I asked Kayato. He nodded.

"For the past two days I haven't been myself" I said to Kayato. "I'm usually a calm, nice person; I guess I'm just confused about . . . ." I stopped myself before I said Prince Jai's name.

Kayato tilted his head to the side. "About your feelings for the Prince." Kayato finished my sentence for me.

I looked at the ground, seriously what was wrong with me? I thought I'd better change the subject. I looked at him. "What's going to happen to me?" I asked him. "I mean yesterday I took off without asking your permission again and I didn't come home until late."

"Nothing is going to happen to you, and May-Lyn is fine." He assured me.

"So her father did catch up with her?" I asked confused.

"Yes." He answered. "When I went looking for you yesterday I saw him at the North markets."

"So yesterday when May-Lyn and I were sitting on the stone wall it was you who we saw?" I asked him.

"Yes it was me."

I just nodded because I didn't know what to say.

We didn't train today Kayato said I could have the day off. So I went back to my bedroom to have a lie down and then focused on the first bit of the conversation Kayato and I just had. Kayato's words echoed in my head: *When I yelled at you yesterday I didn't mean to. I'm not normally like that.*

I thought about my parents and Prince Jai. I thought of May-Lyn and Jiro, Ema and Akashi. I lied down and looked up at the ceiling. *I wonder did Prince Jai get my letter.* Just then the front door opened.

"Daddy." Monikku sounded excited.

"Monikku." Kayato's voice replied.

I remembered when I was six and my father came home from work and I ran at him as he just came through the front door, he knelt down to pick me up he hugged me tight. I flashed back to when that happened. Snowbell came into my room, I turned so I facing the door way. I put my left hand down and she walked up to it and sniffed it. I smiled and then I picked her up and she sat on my bed. *Should she be on the bed?* I then quickly picked her up and got up and put her in her bed, then she walked around in a circle then she yawned and lied down.

Just then I got interrupted by tapping on my bedroom window. I slowly moved my head and body to the window. *Jai!* I screamed in my head. I got up and opened the window. He smiled at me; I just looked at him confused.

"Anna." Jai said.

I tried to talk but I couldn't, I was confused and surprised at the same time, this is the second time he had visited me. "Jai." I whispered to him.

Just then Dean came down the hallway; I quickly spun around so I had my back to the Prince. Dean stopped at my doorway and looked at me.

"Anna." Dean said.

"Dean." I replied.

"Is everything okay?" He asked.

"Yep, everything is okay."

He nodded and then started to walk away.

"Dean." I called as he started to turn away. He stopped and turned around.

"Yes?"

"Sorry about yesterday, I didn't mean to yell at you. I'm just confused." I said.

"About Prince Jai." Dean replied.

I didn't know if Jai was still at the window, if he was what was I going to tell him? It wouldn't be right for Royalty to date a peasant but Jiro isn't Royalty and he's dating May-Lyn. But it was true I do have feelings for Prince Jai.

"I guess so." I said, hoping that he would change the subject.

He nodded. "It's okay Anna." He said with a smile on his face. Then he walked away.

After I made sure he was gone, I turned to the window. To my surprise Jai was still standing there with the biggest smile on his face. *Great he heard the conversation. What am I going to do now?*

"I got your letter." He said.

"You did?" I asked happily.

He nodded. Then held out a piece of paper, I took it from his hand.

"Read it, but not until I go, okay?" Jai informed me.

"Okay."

He smiled and then looked at me. "Bye." He said.

"Bye Jai."

I watched him get on his horse and take off. I then closed the window and sat down on my bed and swung my legs so they were on the bed and then I moved my body so I was sitting on side which was facing the door way. I unfolded the letter and started reading it:

Dear Anna,
Thank you for your letter. I didn't realise you had visited me until I went to bed that night. I miss you a lot too, Mia misses you too. I wish you were still living in the palace. In your letter you were you honest, I like that about you. How is your training going? I heard that Kayato is the best in the North Region. I can't wait to see you again.
From Prince Jai.

I was happy that the Prince got my letter and that he wrote one back to me. He had fantastic handwriting, I smiled to myself. Should I write him one back? I wasn't sure, but in his letter he did say that he can't wait to see me again. *I will write one back to him, but not straight away, I'll wait a day.* Just then Yasumi came into my bedroom.

"Hi Anna." She said.

"Hey Yasumi." I said with a smile.

"I hope you didn't mind that Monikku and I borrowed Snowbell for the day." Her soft voice said.

"No, its okay, I don't mind." I assured her.

She smiled, then looked at my hand and a bigger smile came to her face. I smiled back. Then she walked away. I wanted to tell Prince Jai that I love him, but I don't know if I should tell him in person or on paper. We all were at the kitchen table having dinner that Saturday night, Monikku was chewing on her dinner when she looked at Emika's hand and her mouth dropped open, Taro was still standing up leaned over his little sister and put his index finger under her chin and lightly closed Monikku's mouth. *How rich was Kayato, seriously?* Monikku then turned her head to face Taro; he sat down beside her and started to eat his dinner. I smiled to myself. It was after dinner when Kayato started to speak.

"Taro, I need to talk to you alone." Kayato said.

Taro looked at his father. "Okay." Taro sounded a bit nervous.

They both got up and walked into the garden. We were all watching them. You could see Kayato talking to Taro. Taro smiled and said something to Kayato. *I wonder does Yasumi know that Kayato brought Taro and Emika a house.* They made their way back up the steps and into the kitchen. Taro was still smiling, walked over to Emika and lightly grabbed her hand, she got up and they both walked outside into the garden. Once again we all watched. Taro talked to Emika, after Taro told her he picked Emika up and hugged her. After I helped with the washing up I went to my bedroom and grabbed my night kimono and headed for the bathroom. I then headed back to my bedroom and sat down on my bed, Snowbell was sitting up in her bed I smiled at her. I started to think about Prince Jai again. So I got some paper and a pen from my luggage and made my way out to the kitchen table and sat down and began writing:

To Jai,
Thanks for your letter. My training is going good, how is your sister? I want to tell you something but would it be wrong of me to say so? I want to tell you so badly. I miss seeing you every day, like we use to.
From Anna.

I got up from the kitchen table with the letter and pen in my hand and made my way back into my bedroom. I put the letter and pen down on the bedside table, pulled back the covers of my bed, turned my light off and got in bed and went to sleep.

Next morning I woke up to Snowbell barking. "Snowbell." I said.

I looked to where her bed was, she wasn't in there I quickly threw the cover off, got up and rushed to the hallway, she was standing there barking. I picked her up and slowly made my way to the kitchen the kitchen, but I stopped at the corner of the hallway and poked my head around the corner, to my shock four of the South palace officers were standing in Kayato's kitchen. *What do they want?* I then quickly made my way back to my bedroom and got into my bed and put Snowbell under the covers, I made sure she was on left side of the bed.

"Snowbell, lie down." I told her.

While May-Lyn and I were working for King Jou and found Snowbell on the beach, we taught her some tricks such as lie down, sit, stay. She lied down. Then footsteps started to come down the hallway. *Shoot, what about Snowbell's bed,* I quickly grabbed it and shoved it in the wardrobe and stuck my suitcase in front of it and quickly dashed back in my bed. I shut my eyes and slowly opened them as if I was just waking up when two of the guards along with Kayato came bursting in the room. Snowbell was still lying down.

"What's happening?" I asked as I sat up.

"The dog you left in Princess Mia's care has run off." The older officer replied.

I knew who he was, Kanjo, the officer who arrested me for talking to Prince Jai without King Jou's permission. While May-Lyn and I were working for King Jou, whenever we saw Kanjo he didn't smile. I don't think he ever does.

"What do you want me to do about it?" I asked. *And they are only coming to see me now; it has been days since she has been here, unless the Princess didn't say anything until now.*

"Do you know where she is?" The younger officer asked.

"No, I have no idea where she could be." I lied. *Snowbell don't you move.*

"You're lying." Kanjo said.

"Why would I lie, I have no reason to lie." I assured him.

"Search the room" Kanjo said to younger officer "You two out." Kanjo said rudely.

I got up, and lightly pulled the cover down, I then walked to the kitchen with Kayato on the right side of me. *Shoot, the letters!* Great if they look at them.

"Sorry for all this." I said to Kayato.

"It's okay; we have to go out to the back veranda." He said.

We made our way to the back veranda to where Yasumi, Taro, Emika, Monikku, Dean, Shi-Lou and Jin and the other two South palace guards were. Everybody was sitting down expect for the two South palace guards. Kayato went to sit beside Yasumi; Monikku was sitting on the other side of her and Dean, and Taro and Emika, then Shi-Lou and Jin. I sat down next to Jin, Monikku looked like she was about to cry' I don't blame her either. Kayato had a hold of Yasumi's hand, I looked at Taro's hand and he had a hold of Emika's hand. *How long is this going to take?*

Finally both Kanjo and the younger officer came to the back veranda. *Where the heck is Snowbell?*

"Sorry for wasting your time this morning Kayato." Said the younger officer that was with Kanjo.

"It's okay." Kayato said.

The younger officer nodded and turned and walked out to the front door, he was followed by the other two guards standing up. Kanjo glared at me. And then walked towards me, grabbed my wrist and yanked me up.

"What are you doing?" I asked him.

"King Jou would like to speak to you."

"I'm not going anywhere with you." I assured him.

"Yes you are!" Then he pulled me along.

"So King Jou would like to speak to me in my night kimono, would he?" I asked.

Kanjo then stopped, and looked me. "Go and get changed then."

I quickly walked to my bedroom, grabbed my orange kimono and headed for the bathroom; after I got changed I slowly cleaned my teeth. And made my way back to the back veranda, where Kanjo and Kayato's family, Dean, Shi-Lou and Jin still were sitting.

"It's about time." Kanjo muttered.

If I could roll my eyes I would have, then he grabbed my wrist and pulled me to Kayato's front door. On our way past the kitchen, I heard:

"Daddy." Monikku's little voice sounded frightened.

"Everything is going to be okay." He said to her.

Kanjo opened the front door and to my surprise King Jou was standing a few feet away from the front steps, the other three guards were near his white horse which is actually called a grey was to his left side but a few feet away. *Great, what does he want?* I felt sicker. He was dressed in red with gold around the collar and sleeves. Kanjo led me down the steps; I didn't have my sword with me so if it was duel he wants he won't be getting one. We walked two feet towards King Jou and stopped, Kanjo than let go of my wrist.

"Anna." King Jou said.

I looked at him, his brown eyes fixed on me, his black hair neatly brushed.

"You're Highness." I replied bluntly.

King Jou smiled, I didn't smile back I had better things to do with my time then smile to King Jou. Then all of a sudden he stopped smiling. *Seriously what did he want?*

"Do you know where Snowbell is?" He said calmly.

"No Your Highness, I don't know where she is." I lied to his face. Then I started to walk back into the house.

"Thank you for your time Anna." The King said.

I didn't answer him, I just kept walking, and I heard the horse's hooves going down the road. *Great now I got to wait until tomorrow to give Jai the letter.*

I made my way back to back veranda, I past Shi-Lou and Jin on the way, they didn't look happy. Then I saw Monikku with Snowbell, but she looked different somehow. Snowbell's fur was shorter and she had a dog coat on? Did she have that on when I put her under the covers? And she also had a collar on, but when I got closer to Snowbell the coat was like her fur but brown. No wonder I didn't get arrested, because Monikku put on Snowbell a coat that looked like real fur, but actually it was fake fur. That's why May-Lyn and I called her Snowbell, because of her white fur.

Training was off for today, so I went out to the front and practice my forward flips and back flips. I did that until lunch time. I decided I would go and see Prince Jai that night, I couldn't wait to till tomorrow and after all he said in his letter he couldn't wait to see me either.

The afternoon past quickly and we were having dinner, Snowbell was lying down next to Monikku's chair, the coat Monikku put on her was off. After dinner I quickly washed up and headed to my bedroom grabbed my night kimono and headed for the bathroom, I then quickly had a shower and cleaned my teeth. I went back to my bedroom and lied down. I reached over to the bedside table and grabbed my letter to Prince Jai and put it under my pillow, I then got up and put the pen back with my luggage.

I waited about an hour after everybody had gone to bed, I put my sword on. I got the letter and stuck it in the sleeve of my night kimono then I quietly headed towards the front door. I waited on the front veranda for about forty-five minutes until my night vision started to work. I slowly made my way down the front steps and headed towards the

South palace. It was full moon out tonight, which was good and also bad. I could easily get caught for sneaking into the palace which was the bad thing, but the good thing was that it was easier to see when walking.

I finally came to the wooden bridge, I slowly crossed it and made my way up to the palace wall, I poked my head around the corner, this time there was only one guard. I pulled my head back and grabbed four small stones in my left hand. I threw two and the guard went to look at what the noise was. I quickly ran to the front door and opened them, I made my way down the first hallway, stopped at the corner and poked my head around the corner, and there was no guard. Just to be sure I slowly made my way down the second hallway and to Prince Jai's room. I finally reached Jai's golden door, when somebody's hand grabbed my wrist from behind I gasped.

"Anna." It was Prince Jai's voice.

"Jai." I said in relief.

He opened his bedroom door with his free hand, and then he moved his hand from my wrist so that his hand was holding my hand. He then led me into his bedroom; we walked over to his bed and sat down.

"How are you?" He whispered.

"Good and how are you?"

"Same." He smiled.

Then all of a sudden he pulled me closer to him, I looked at the ground then he moved my hair so it was behind my right ear, not hanging down and hiding my face. *I love you Prince Jai.* I want to tell him. I pulled out the letter from my kimono sleeve and handed it to him. He smiled, I didn't smile back.

"Anna, what's the matter?" He asked.

"Nothing, I better get going." I said as I quickly got up and let go of his hand.

I rushed to his bedroom door and closed it behind me and rushed to the front door. I totally forgot about the guard who was at the front door, I opened it and rushed out. I only remembered he was there when:

"Ay! You stop!" The guard shouted.

Should I stop? Or just keep running, which will be easier? I stopped running. "Good" The guard said. "Now turn around slowly."

I turned around slowly, and the guard walked up to me, I was nervous. I knew this guard also his name is Akihiko, he is nicer than Kanjo, at least with Akihiko if you were caught sneaking into the palace to try and steal something he wouldn't arrest you if you stopped running when he asked you to. May-Lyn and I use to have the night shift with him. I looked at him and he looked at me. I then dropped the two stones I had left in my hand.

"I won't arrest you, Anna" He said. "But I can't just let you go."

I didn't know whether to say thank you. "So what happens now?" I asked him.

"I don't want to do this." He said.

"Huh?" I asked.

"Take you to King Jou." He said.

"Whoa, hang on" I said. "How about if I just tell you what I was doing here? And then could you let me go?"

"Sorry Anna, it doesn't work like that." Akihiko said.

"But King Jou is asleep; you don't want to wake him, now do you?" I asked.

"He doesn't go to bed until late."

I sighed.

"Sorry Anna."

"It's not your fault." I said to him.

He then lightly grabbed my upper arm and started walking back towards the front door. We went along the first hallway and then the second and then around a corner and walked towards a wooden door which was guarded, they opened the door for us and we walked in. The room was huge; there

I could see King Jou sitting on his golden throne. He was reading something when we came into the room. King Jou had his red and gold kimono on. We walked towards him a bit but then stopped.

"You're Highness." Akihiko said.

King Jou looked up from what he was reading, looked at Akihiko and then looked at me. I looked at the floor. "Yes?" King Jou asked.

"I caught her sneaking out the front door, Your Highness."

King Jou then got up from his seat and walked a few steps towards us then he stopped. Akihiko then let go of my arm. I looked at King Jou and he looked me. *I just should of kept running, why didn't I. Great now Kayato is going to be really mad at me and this time he will mean to yell at me.*

"Why are you here?" King Jou asked.

I can't tell him that I was here to see his son. I was just about to answer him when the doors burst open. I didn't want to see who it was.

"She was here to see me." Jai's voice sounded a few feet behind Akihiko and me.

Great now he's going to be in trouble as well. *I should have just kept running.* King Jou looked past me and focused on his son.

"What?" King Jou sounded confused. He then focused back on me; I didn't want to look at him I just wanted to run to Jai so he could hug me. I forced myself to look at King Jou.

"Is this true?" He asked me.

"Yes, You're Highness." I answered him.

King Jou just looked at me and then walked out of the room. We waited about five minutes; he didn't come back into the room. So Akihiko and Jai walked me back to the front door, Jai handed me a piece of folded paper I put it in my sleeve of my kimono. I said bye to Prince Jai and Akihiko. I made my way back to Kayato's house.

As I came to the front steps of Kayato's house I felt so tired, I nearly fell up the top step. I didn't hurry to my bed I wanted to see what the time was, I quietly made my way to the kitchen and looked at the clock, and the time was 12:00 am on Monday morning. I made my way back to my bedroom, threw the covers back got comfy and fell asleep.

Chapter 6

Telling Prince Jai

It wasn't until midday when I finally woke up, I remembered Prince Jai's letter, and I took it out of my kimono sleeve and put it on the bedside table. I got up grabbed my light green kimono and headed for the bathroom. I finally came out of the bathroom I put my night kimono on my bed and walked out into the kitchen. I didn't want to face Kayato, maybe if I walk back to my bedroom and just stay there. I was about to turn and head back to my bedroom when Kayato called out to me.

"Anna." Kayato said.

"Yes Kayato." I said a bit nervous.

"Please have a seat."

I turned myself around and went back to the kitchen and sat down, I looked at Kayato. I think my heart missed a beat, he didn't look happy at all. *I wish this bit was dream.*

"What were you thinking?!" He said to me.

What I was thinking, I was thinking about Prince Jai. Should I tell him that or would that only make him madder? "I went for a walk." I lied. Wait, what am I doing? First of all I tell Monikku not to lie, because that only makes things more difficult and then I lie. *Great.*

"Going for a walk to see Prince Jai." Kayato said.

"Yeah." Well I suppose it really wasn't a lie that time; I did go for a walk to see the Prince.

"Look, if you want to go and see Prince Jai, make sure next time you go during the daytime." He said.

"So King Jou did tell you about what happened last night?" I asked confused.

"No, Akihiko stopped by this morning to make sure you made it back okay last night. I had no idea what he was talking about so he told me. He got a shock when I told him I didn't know anything about you being at the palace." He said.

"Sorry I just—" I stopped myself before I said Prince Jai's name.

Kayato looked at me, I looked at the table. "You're going to be punished." He informed me.

This made me look at him. I don't like that word *Punish.*

"Okay." I managed to say.

"For two weeks you're going to be on the night shift, starting tonight at nine pm and your shift will end at two am guarding my house." Kayato informed me.

"Okay."

I made my way back to my bedroom; Kayato said I had the rest of the day off, until 9:00 pm tonight. I sat down on my bed and grabbed Prince Jai's letter and then lied down on my right side and started to read it:

Dear Anna,
Just tell me please, it wouldn't be wrong of you to tell me. Mia is good. I'm going to visit you on Thursday night, so you can tell me whatever you need to tell me, okay. I miss seeing you everyday too.
From Jai.

I folded the letter and put it back on my bedside table, Thursday Prince Jai was going to visit me and that was three days time. Ugh I wished May-Lyn was here, I could talk to her about this. I fell back asleep.

It was night when I woke up, I went to the bathroom with my night kimono and had a shower and walked out into the kitchen, good it was only 7:00 pm. I quietly ate my dinner; I washed up and headed to the bathroom to clean my teeth. I thought of my parents. I sighed and walked back out into the kitchen. Monikku was in the lounge sitting down on the floor, Snowbell was sitting beside her. Monikku picked up Snowbell and hugged her. I smiled.

I then walked out on the back veranda Kayato was sitting at the round table, he didn't say anything to me, so I sat beside him he moved his eyes so they looked at me for a split second and then he focused back on the garden.

"I guess you're mad at me too." I said.

He looked me. "No." He said.

I sighed, what was I going to do for next hour and half? We just sat there for a bit without saying a word. I thought of Prince Jai, Akashi and my Grandparents.

"Do your Grandparent's like Japan?" Kayato asked randomly.

"Yeah they do."

The time past quickly and Monikku came out to the veranda. "Daddy."

"Monikku." Kayato said.

He picked her up and she sat on his lap, he then stood up still holding Monikku. Monikku had her head over his shoulder and said good night to me. I said good night to her, I smiled then Yasumi came from the hallway and Kayato handed her Monikku then the three of them walked to Monikku's room. I smiled to myself and remembered when my parents would do that. I then walked into the kitchen to see what the time was; it was only eight-thirty pm. Maybe if I start early, that shouldn't matter. I then walked back to the veranda and sat down again. I flashed back to when May-Lyn, Ema and I were working for King Jou, May-Lyn, Ema and I would talk while we were meant to be looking to see if anybody was trying to break into the palace. One night we were mucking around Ema was hiding in some bushes which were near the palace entrance. I was guarding the door, May-Lyn was walking past the bushes, and I knew Ema was hiding in there, and as May-Lyn walked past Ema jumped out and scared her. May-Lyn screamed so loud. After she stopped screaming we all burst out laughing. I sighed I missed those days and smiled to myself.

I got up and walked around the front, I stayed there for a bit, I then walked to the back veranda I really needed to go to the toilet. I quickly dashed off to the bathroom. I then went to the kitchen to check the clock; gee the time past quickly it was now 12:00 am. I then walked to the front, creak went the floor board. Oops I then quickly rushed to the front door and made my way outside. I stayed on duty until 2:30 am that Tuesday morning. I walked slowly back to my bedroom and put my sword in its case, lied down on my bed and fell asleep.

Once again I woke up at midday, I fell out of bed I got up and grabbed my dark pink kimono and headed for the bathroom. I made my way out into the kitchen where Kayato and his family and Dean were having lunch. I ate a small bowl of rice I didn't feel like eating much.

"I washed your kimonos Anna." Yasumi's soft voice said.

"Thank you."

"No worries." She said with a smile.

I smiled weakly; I didn't feel like doing anything at all. Actually I felt sick. I went out the front to get some fresh air, and then I walked back in because I forgot my sword, after I got my sword I returned to the front. *I don't think I can do the night shift.* What was wrong with me? Should I tell Kayato I can't do the night shift? No I better not do that. The afternoon past quickly and I didn't even realise until Dean came to tell me it was dinner.

"Anna." Dean called from the front veranda.

I looked in his direction. "Yes?" I asked him.

"Dinner is ready." He answered my question.

"Okay." I said as I slowly got up from where I was sitting under a tree. I made my way up the front steps.

"Hey, are you okay?" Dean asked.

"Yep." I said as I finally got up the last step.

He looked at me worried. We walked into the house and headed for the kitchen. I sat down between Monikku and Dean, I ate very little that night, and I went to lie back down before I started my night shift. I closed my eyes for a bit and then opened them, I walked out to the kitchen and the time said it was 9:30 pm. *Great now I'm late for night duty.* I quickly walked out the front, I stayed out there for ages and then I walked to the back veranda and walked down the steps and sat down on the stone wall, just then Kayato came down the steps.

"We're going to bed now." He said.

I looked at him. "Okay." I said weakly.

"Is everything okay?" He asked.

"I think so" I said. "Please go to sleep."

Kayato looked at me and smiled and then walked off back into the house.

It was nearly sun rise on Thursday morning when someone'jumped over the stone wall; I pulled my sword out of its scabbard and got up. The person walked towards me.

"Anna." The person said.

"What?" I asked.

"Anna, it's me Jai."

"Oh."

He kept walking towards me and lightly grabbed my hand, I put my sword'back in its scabbard and I just stood there looking into his eyes.

"What do you need to tell me?" He asked.

"I love you." I answered him.

"I love you too" He said back to me. "I haven't stopped thinking about you since you left the palace."

I smiled weakly and then fell down. Jai still had a hold of me and knelt down beside me.

"Whoa, Anna are you okay?"

"No." I answered him.

He then picked me up in his arms and started to carry me back to the house.

"Jai, you don't have to do this." I said weakly.

"I'm not going to leave you out here."

He slowly carried me up the steps. *Damn he's strong.* I stretched my hand and opened the door for us, I looked at Jai and he smiled at me.

"Where's your bedroom?" He said softly.

"Keep walking, till you reach a hallway and it's the first door on the left hand side." I barely got the words out.

We came to the hallway and Jai walked to my bedroom and then he walked up to my bed and slowly put me on the bed. I moved my legs over so he could sit down. He sat down and stretched out his hand and lightly grabbed my hand.

"I'll go and get help." He said.

"No, wait till Kayato or someone else wakes up." I said.

"Okay."

Just then I heard footsteps out in the kitchen, Jai heard them too. He looked at me and I nodded. Jai let go of my hand and got up and walked out into the kitchen.

"Kayato." I heard Jai say.

"You're Highness." Kayato's voice sounded shocked.

I don't blame Kayato for being shocked one minute the Prince isn't standing in your kitchen then the next minute he is.

"It's Anna, she collapsed."

Just then Kayato rushed into my bedroom with Jai right behind him. He looked at me. "Anna." His voice sounded concern.

I didn't say a word, just then we were interrupted when a masked man smashed through the window he pulled out a knife and threw it at me. I waited for the knife to pierce my skin, I had my eyes closed, and nothing had happened. *Am I dead?* I opened my eyes to find Jai still standing up and Kayato's sword at my neck, just then something went *Ping!* I moved my eyes and looked at the sheet. There was the knife lying on the sheet. I tried to move, but I couldn't.

The masked man had gone, and by the looks of it he threw a smoke bomb so he could escape.

"I'll tell Shi-Lou and Jin to be on the lookout." Kayato said. I looked at Kayato and he leaned over me to pick up the knife and went.

"Jai." I said weakly.

He looked at me.

"Are you okay?" I asked.

"Yes." He replied.

I smiled weakly at him. "You better get home" I said. "Your father will be looking for you."

"I'm not leaving you." Prince Jai said again.

"Please Jai; I don't want you to get into trouble."

"Don't worry about that."

Just then Kayato came back into my room; he didn't have the knife in his hand. He sat down next to me. I didn't know what to do now so I just looked at him. "Thank you." I managed to say to Kayato.

"It's okay" Kayato's Cantonese accent said. "You need to rest for a couple of days, so no more training for the moment and diffidently no more night shifts for you."

"Okay." I said weakly. I smiled and then I thought of Snowbell. "Where is Snowbell?" I asked Kayato.

"She's in Monikku's room" Kayato assured me. "Now get some rest."

"Okay." I said.

He then got up and walked out, Jai then sat beside me. He lightly grabbed my hand and squeezed it, I looked at our hands.

"What about the broken glass?" I asked Jai.

"I'll clean it up; do you know where a dust pan is?"

"There is one in the bathroom; it's just to the left."

He leaned his head in and lightly kissed my cheek, then he let go of my hand and got up and walked to the bathroom. A couple of seconds later he came back with the dustpan walked around the foot of my bed and went over to the broken glass, he cleaned up the broken glass and left to empty the dustpan a couple minutes went by and he came back empty handed. He sat down on my bed. *I finally told Prince Jai that I love him.* He lightly grabbed my hand and squeezed it again. I smiled and he smiled back. *How long will I be resting for? How long before King Jou comes to Kayato's house and bursts in the front door?* I stopped thinking about that and focused on Jai.

"Sorry about the other night." I said.

He looked at me. "Don't worry about it Anna." He said.

I wanted to hug him, but Kayato said I had to rest. Just then I heard footsteps coming down the hallway. *Uh oh,* thank goodness it was only Monikku, she stopped at the door way and looked in my direction and she walked up to the bed and hugged me.

"Hey." I said.

"Anna." Her little voice said.

She than let go of me, just then more footsteps came down the hallway. It was Taro.

"Monikku." He said firmly.

Monikku spun around to face her older brother and looked at him.

"You heard what Dad said, Anna needs to rest." He said.

"Okay." She sighed. Then she walked up to Taro and they walked down the hallway.

"Cute kid." Prince Jai said.

"Yeah, she is." I said with a smile.

At this point I was sitting up, but I still had my legs lying down, Prince Jai moved a bit closer. I didn't know what to do, so I just stayed still.

"What about your father?" I asked quickly.

"If he does come here to look for me, I'll tell him I was here to see you, which is true."

"Okay." I replied.

He leaned his face in closer to mine, he was still holding my hand, and our foreheads touched. I closed my eyes and so did Prince Jai. I moved my head in slightly. We were about to kiss when we were interrupted by banging on the door. I quickly opened my eyes. *Great that will probably be King Jou.*

"Jai." I said quietly.

He also had his eyes opened.

"You better go" I said. "I've already caused enough trouble."

He was about to say something when footsteps came down the hallway. I wanted to hide somewhere. Just then Kanjo along with King Jou stood at the door way, I quickly let go of Prince Jai's hand.

"What's going on here?" King Jou asked.

"I'm here to see Anna." The Prince replied.

Prince Jai got up from my bed and walked out the door. King Jou followed, Kanjo glared at me. *What are you looking at?* I could have said it to him, but I thought I'd better keep my mouth shut. After he looked at me he walked out. I felt like I was going to throw up. I wish May-Lyn was here she is never around when I need her. I then lied back down, I thought of Jai and how much trouble he would be in. I bet he would be guarded at all times from now on. I closed my eyes and tried'to force myself to go to sleep but it was no use, it was daylight. So I just lied in bed. The time moved slowly. Great only if I didn't sneak into his bedroom none of this wouldn't have happened. I slowly got up; I stretched and nearly fell over. I walked to the kitchen and came back to my bedroom.

After I came back from the kitchen I noticed a folded piece of paper on my bed. *Am I losing my mind? That wasn't there before was it? Or maybe Jai left it here, and I hadn't noticed because maybe he was sitting on it? Ugh.* I lightly kneeled down and rested my arms on the bed and unfolded the piece of paper and started reading it:

Dear Anna,
I love you; meet me in Kayato's garden at 10:00 pm tonight.
Love Jai.

I put the letter on the bedside table and climbed back in bed, what if it was a trap. What if Jai only said that he loved me to make me feel secure? Oh well only one way to find out.

Night had fallen and everybody had gone to sleep, but I lied in bed wide awake. I slowly got up and made my way to the kitchen, and walked to the door that led to the back veranda. I slowly made my way down the steps just then somebody jumped over the stone wall. I froze but then realised it was only Jai. I walked over to him and then stopped he hugged me lightly and then he let me go.

"Anna." He whispered.

"You're Highness."

He looked at me surprised. "Anna, you know you don't have to call me that."

"I know."

He lightly grabbed my hand and he walked over to the stone wall and we sat down. I didn't know if I should say anything or just keep my mouth shut, I decided to keep my mouth shut. It would be better if I did. Jai moved a bit closer, I looked at him and he smiled I smiled weakly at him. I rested my head on his shoulder but then I quickly moved my head off and looked at the ground. *What am I doing? He is Royalty after all.* Prince Jai put his pointer finger under my chin and lightly moved my face towards his face and then he took his finger away.

"You're beautiful." The Prince said.

I didn't know what to say. "You're handsome." I suddenly blurted out.

He then pulled me closer to him; he moved his arm down to my lower back. I sat there looking at him.

"Earlier today when we were in my bedroom you were about to say something, but then we got interrupted by Kanjo and your father" I said then paused. "What were you going to say? If you don't mind me asking?"

"I was going to say" He paused. "You haven't caused any trouble."

"But I broke the law." I replied.

"No, you haven't" He said firmly. "The law about peasants speaking to the South Royal Family and needs my father's permission first it's stupid" He paused again. "My father shouldn't have had you arrested for talking to me without his permission."

"Sorry." I said. *Great there I go again me and my big mouth.*

"Don't be sorry." The Prince said.

He then moved his other arm so it was around my stomach and his hand on my lower back he slightly moved it so both his hands were linked together. I then again rested my head on his shoulder. *What was the time?*

"Jai."

"Yes?"

"I better get some sleep."

"Okay, I'll walk you to your bedroom."

His hands than unwrapped from my waist and he took my hand. And we both stood up. We walked slowly up the steps I opened the door and Jai closed it behind him. We then past the kitchen and walked down the hallway to my bedroom, I tried to find the light switch and finally turned it on. Gee it was bright. I turned to him and let go of his hand. He hugged me. When he finally let me go, we both looked into each other's eyes.

"I love you." The Prince said.

"I love you too." I said with a smile.

"Bye."

I didn't want to say bye, but I forced myself to. "Bye Jai"

He turned and went, I waited a bit then I pulled back the covers of my bed I turned off the light and made my way to bed I got in and got comfy but I couldn't get off to sleep. I just stayed awake. It was probably just before dawn when I got to sleep.

When I finally woke up on Friday morning, I slowly got up and headed towards the kitchen. I was hungry; I really needed to eat something. I came to the kitchen and walked up to the fridge. There was a bowl of rice, I grabbed it from the fridge, and I didn't worry about heating it up. I grabbed some chopsticks from the drawer, sat down and started eating slowly. While I was chewing I stirred the rice around in the bowl. It took me ages to eat, but I didn't care. After I had finished eating I slowly washed up. And then went to the bathroom to have a shower.

I rested for three days, it was now Monday. Kayato had the window fixed the day after the attack had happen; before he had the window fixed I taped a blanket to the window sill because of the weather. It was morning when I woke up. I made my way slowly to the kitchen; only Kayato and Yasumi were at the kitchen table.

"Morning." I said to Kayato and Yasumi.

Morning." They both said.

I sat down in front of a bowl, and started to eat. "Where's everybody?" I asked.

"Taro's at work, Emika took Monikku to the markets" Kayato said. "And Dean is sleeping."

"Nice." I replied.

After breakfast Kayato and I went outside to train, he didn't waste any time. As soon as he stopped and spun around to face me, he pulled out his sword and rushed at me, I blocked his strike and pulled my sword into an upward strike and rushed at him, he blocked my move. We trained all day; we only had a break when it was lunch time.

Chapter 7

What's with Taro?

The sun was setting and Taro walked into the kitchen, he didn't look happy I noticed that he had a piece of paper in his hand; he didn't say anything to me. I don't think he'noticed that I was sitting at the table, he walked straight past me and walked onto the back veranda and sat down on the top step. *What's going on?* Just then Emika and Monikku came into the kitchen.

"Hey Anna." Emika said.

"Hey."

Monikku walked out to Taro, she sat beside him, and he then put his arm around her little back.

"Is Taro okay?" Emika asked.

"I don't know, he walked straight past me when he came into the kitchen." I replied.

I looked at Emika and she had a worried look on her face. I don't blame her for being worried. Monikku came back inside; Taro looked behind him and then smiled. Just then Kayato came into the kitchen, I looked at Taro and his smile was gone. Emika then walked out to Taro, she sat beside him. Monikku went to her bedroom. Kayato looked at me.

"Is everything okay with Taro?" He asked.

"I don't know."

Everybody was sitting at the kitchen table having dinner, everybody except Taro. He was sitting in the lounge. Whatever happened he didn't want to talk about it.

After dinner I went to the bathroom to have a shower and clean my teeth. I walked back into the kitchen and sat down, I guess everybody was out the front, but Taro was still sitting in the lounge. I thought of Jai. Just then Taro came into the kitchen and also sat down. He still had the piece of paper in his hand. He looked at me blankly.

"I got fired from my job." He said.

"What happened?" I asked.

"It doesn't matter" He said. "And now Emika and I will have to wait a bit longer to get married."

"And you don't want to tell your Dad that you lost your job?"

"What do you expect he will say? Taro asked.

I had no answer for his question. I didn't want to make matters worse.

"If I was you, I would just tell him what happened and why you lost your job." I said.

Taro didn't say anything. Kayato came into the kitchen; Taro stood up and walked over to his father.

"Here." Taro said and handed Kayato the piece of paper.

Kayato took the piece of paper from Taro, Taro then walked off. Kayato watched his son leave the room and then looked at the piece of paper then he looked at me. I just stared at him. Kayato then walked into the lounge and sat down; I decided I better get to bed.

I woke up early the next morning; I grabbed my light brown kimono. I didn't really like this kimono, but I thought I better wear it and headed to the bathroom to get dress. I chucked my night kimono on my bed as I past, I made my way out to the kitchen, Taro was sitting on the back step again, I bet he couldn't sleep last night, I sat down. I thought of Akashi. I went back to my bedroom, to put my sword on and made my way out to the kitchen once again. I looked into the lounge room and on the coffee table was the piece of paper. *Did Kayato read it?*

Dean then came into the kitchen. "Morning Anna." He said.

"Morning."

He then sat down at the kitchen table, and looked at Taro and then focused back on me, I walked up to a seat and sat down. *What's going to happen now? Did Taro tell Emika that he lost his job?* Monikku came into the kitchen, she yawned and I pulled a chair out for her to sit down on. She looked so cute sitting there. She then turned her little head and looked outside.

"Is Taro okay?" Her little voice asked.

"No." Dean answered her.

She looked at Dean and then looked at Taro. Just then Yasumi came into the kitchen. Monikku looked to see who it was.

"Mummy." She said. She got off her seat and walked up to Yasumi, she smiled.

"Morning sweetie" Yasumi said.

Monikku then put her arms around Yasumi's legs, Yasumi leant down and picked her up and they walked to the fridge. Monikku helped by opening the door for Yasumi.

"Thanks Monikku." Yasumi said.

Emika and Taro had breakfast on the back veranda; Kayato didn't say anything, I just sat there eating my breakfast, Monikku was stirring her breakfast and then she would eat some and stir it again like most little kids do. Snowbell found her way into the kitchen, she sat down next to Monikku's chair and looked at me. Then she lied down.

After breakfast and the dishes were done Yasumi, Monikku and Emika went out the front, Dean went outside, and I followed because I had nothing better to do. Dean and I sat down on the stone wall. By this time Kayato had made his way onto the back veranda and sat down next to his son. Taro didn't say a word, I guessed he was nervous. Kayato then said something to Taro, Taro looked at his father; he still didn't say a word, Taro then looked back at the table. I saw Taro's mouth move, but he still didn't look at his father.

A couple of minutes went by and Kayato and Taro were still talking, then all of a sudden they both got up Kayato hugged Taro. Taro made his way back into the kitchen and Kayato made his way down to us. I thought of May-Lyn and Jiro and wondering when would see them again.

I went back to training, Dean was beside me. It was a two on one duel. It felt weird to have Dean by my side by but it felt good almost like I was invincible. Dean and I bowed to Kayato; we trained for most of the day. It felt like my hand was going to drop off. After we had lunch we went back outside to train some more, but this time was different. Kayato handed me another sword, I took it from him. *Am I ready for this?* Before I could answer that question Kayato rushed at me, I blocked his strike. We trained until the sun went down. Now both of my hands felt like they were going to drop off.

After dinner I slowly made my way to the bathroom to have a shower. I made my way back to the kitchen and onto the back veranda, and headed towards the stone wall and sat down. I heard the hooves of a horse, then all of a sudden they stopped and next thing May-Lyn jumped over the wall, she lightly landed on her feet, looked at me and sat down.

"Anna." She said.

"May-Lyn." I answered her.

"How have you been?" She asked me.

"Alright." She looked at me; I wanted to tell her so much. She just stared at me.

"May" I started to say. "I . . . ." I stopped talking.

I didn't know what to say to her; so much had happened since the last time we spoke. I decided it would be best if I start with apologising to her because when asked me if everything was okay with Kayato and Dean I lied to her.

"You know how you asked me if everything was okay with Kayato and Dean the last time we spoke." I said to her.

"Yeah."

I didn't want to tell her that I lied to her, great why didn't I just tell her what happened when she asked me.

"I . . . . uh . . . . um" I wanted to tell her but I couldn't get the words out.

"Anna?" She asked.

I took a deep breath. "When you asked me if everything was okay, it wasn't" I said. "Sorry that I lied to you."

She just looked at me, next thing I know she hugs me. After she let go of me I looked at her.

"You're not angry at me?" I asked surprised.

"No."

I better change the subject and fast, once again Jiro wasn't with her. Should I ask her about Jiro, ugh I didn't know what to talk about and yet there was so much to talk about. I looked at her and she smiled.

"How's Jiro?" I asked.

"Yeah he's good, he's spending some time with his parents." May-Lyn answered me.

"Nice." I replied, that's all I could think of.

What should we talk about now? Should I tell her about Prince Jai? I decided not to tell her about the masked man that attacked me and tried to kill me, knowing May-Lyn and being a Princess she probably have the North guards guarding Kayato's house.

"I spoke to Prince Jai." I mumbled.

"What?" She asked.

"I said, I spoke to Prince Jai" I repeated.

"That's great Anna." She said happily.

I smiled at her.

"You know how I told you that I was going to the East." She said.

"Yeah."

"Well I got a surprise for you." She said with that cheeky grin on her face.

"What is it?"

Then all of a sudden someone spoke from behind the stone wall. "Hey Anna." The voice said.

I turned to look to see who said my name; there with her arms leaning on the stone wall was Ema. Wearing her green kimono, her brown eyes looking at me her shoulder-length black hair wasn't tied up.

"Ema!" I said.

She jumped over the stone wall too and landed beside May-Lyn, I stood up then she walked up to me and squeezed me. After she let me go and I could finally breathe again I sat down next to May-Lyn, she sat on the other side of her.

"So, how's the Prince?" Ema asked and she nudged May-Lyn, May-Lyn smiled.

"He's good." I answered her.

"So have you kissed him yet?" She suddenly asked.

This was like Ema, to ask questions like that. But for anyone who didn't know Ema as well as May-Lyn and me, they would get such a shock. May-Lyn learned this the hard way. I introduced May-Lyn to Ema, and Jiro was leaving to go home, because May-Lyn and Jiro didn't kiss. Ema pipes up and says:

"Why didn't you kiss him?"

At the time, they had only been going out for two weeks and now it has been four months since they have been together.

"No Ema, I haven't kissed Prince Jai yet." I answered her.

"Oh." She said sounding disappointed.

We sat there and talked for a bit then they had to go. I made my way back to the house, I looked at the clock it was only 9:00 pm. I decided to go to bed and started to walk when:

"Anna." Kayato's voice suddenly said.

I nearly had a heart attack; I looked to the kitchen table to find Kayato sitting there, *whoa okay, was he sitting there all this time?*

"Yes?" I said slowly.

"How's May-Lyn?" He suddenly blurted out.

I didn't ask how she was, great, some friend I am. "I don't know, I didn't get around to asking her."

He nodded. "Goodnight." He said.

"Okay, goodnight." I replied'

I then headed off to bed; it was good talking to May-Lyn and Ema. As I got comfy I thought of Jai.

Chapter 8

Queen Rira

When I woke up, which seemed like only a short night I grabbed my light pink kimono and headed to the bathroom to get changed. I then went back to my bedroom to put my sword on and my locket and rushed to the kitchen. Everybody was sitting down expect Dean who probably was still asleep. I sat down next to Monikku.

After breakfast Kayato and I went outside, this time he didn't pull out his sword and rush at me. He just stood there, I stood there confused. *Are we waiting for Dean?*

"Excuse me Kayato, but what are we waiting for?" I asked quietly.

He was about to answer and then stopped, just then I heard footsteps coming down the steps, I didn't look I couldn't be bothered, just then a person walked past me, with two guards, I couldn't see who they were because all three of them had armour covering their faces but I could tell where they were from because they had the maroon on. Kayato walked towards me and then turned his body so he was on my right hand side but also facing the three other people who just showed up. Just then Dean joined us; he went to stand on my left hand side.

"Anna met your challengers for today." Kayato suddenly said.

"Oh okay." I said nervously.

Kayato handed me the other sword I had been training with yesterday, before I could say thank you Dean and Kayato took a step back and then the guard on the left rushed at me, the guard took out his sword and swiped at my head, I ducked and then knocked his feet from out under of him with my feet. *No wonder Dean and Kayato took a step back.* The guard got up quickly; I blocked his sword strike and took the tip of it off. The guard then went back to his standing position, and then the guard from the right and the person standing in the middle rushed at me. *So this is why* Kayato *gave me a second sword.* I blocked their strikes which were a bit harder than I thought; we clashed swords for a bit.

"Anna, you do know that you can use karate." Dean said.

"Yeah, but you know what happened the last time I tried that." I answered while blocking sword strikes.

"Yes."

"What happened?" Kayato asked.

"Well May-Lyn and Anna were working for King Jou; they were training for when somebody broke into the palace.

One of the South palace guards pretended to be a thief. Anna caught up to the guard at the South beach, Anna was about to kick the guard in the wrist when he grabbed her ankle and twisted it which than made her flip and she landed in the sand" Dean paused. "King Jou and I were watching to see how well the girls did."

"Oh."

I then knocked the tip off from the second guard's sword, and she went to stand next to the other guard. It was only me and the person who was standing in the middle. We clashed swords for a while and then I knocked the sword out of the person's hand. Just then the person removed the armour to my shock it was Queen Rira, King Jou's wife. Her long black hair fell around her shoulders, her brown eyes looked at me and she smiled. The two guards left their head armour on.

"Your Highness." I said shocked.

"Anna." She said smiling.

Today marked the second month Queen Rira went away and hasn't been back since, until today. The training session was done for today, we all walked back into the house. Queen Rira and I were standing near my bedroom door; she wanted to speak with me alone.

"Anna, I was wondering if you could escort me back to the South Palace." She said.

I was about to answer her when Dean came along.

"What's happening?" Dean asked.

"I just asked Anna if she could escort me back to the South Palace." Queen Rira answered Dean.

"Yep, she can escort you back to the Palace." Dean assured Queen Rira.

"Good, I'll see you out the front in five minutes." Queen Rira said.

She then walked off; I made sure she was out of hearing distance.

"Dean!" I said. "Were you there when King Jou said I wasn't allowed anywhere near the South Palace?"

"Yes, I was there" He said. "But that hasn't stopped you."

"If I'm not back in three hours, check all the local jails, okay." I said.

I then hurried to the front door and opened the door and headed down the steps, Queen Rira was with her grey horse and one of the guards were waiting on their horse, and standing next to them was my horse. I quickly climbed on and we started our way to the South Palace, we were on the dirt path. I was on the right outer side, Queen Rira was in the middle and the other guard was on her other side.

"How have you been?" Queen Rira said.

"Yeah good" I answered her. "And how have you been, Your Highness?"

"Same." She answered me.

"So does King Jou know about your martial art skill?" I asked Queen Rira.

She looked at me. "No he doesn't, that's why I went away for a month to train" Queen Rira answered. "Can you please not say anything; I would like to tell him myself."

"Sure." I answered her.

Just then the left sleeve of my kimono moved showing the white bandage Kayato had wrapped around the scar for me. Queen Rira noticed this.

"What happened there?" She asked me.

"My first duel, I wasn't watching and the swordsman got my arm." I answered her. Well it wasn't a lie, King Jou was a swordsman.

"Oh."

"Where is the second guard?" I asked her.

"I told the other guard to go ahead to tell Jou of my arrival."

"Oh okay."

We rode for a bit longer and then we came to the wooden bridge and not very far was the South Palace, I stopped at the bridge but Queen Rira and the guard kept going but then they suddenly stopped, Queen Rira turned her horse around and looked at me.

"Anna?" She asked. "What's the matter?"

"I not only train at Kayato's house I also live there" I answered. "I better get back."

I turned my horse around and headed back to Kayato's house. I made my way down the dirt path; I was glad that Queen Rira was back.

After I got back to Kayato's house I headed to the stables. Unsaddled my horse and washed him, after this I headed back inside Kayato's house. I looked at the clock in the kitchen, it was 11:00 am, and I didn't know what to do, so I went to my bedroom to have a lie down. *This morning was busy, I had a duel with Queen Rira and two guards, and then I escorted her back to the South Palace, what will happen next?* I rolled over to my left side.

It wasn't until the afternoon I got up from my bed I took off my locket, and made my way out to the kitchen.

The months flew by; it had been five months since I have been staying with Kayato and his family.

Chapter 9

The Truth

It was the beginning of a new a month and also marked the seventh month I was living at Kayato's house and his family and along with Dean. Next morning I woke up; I just lied in bed I didn't want to get up. I got bored of just lying there so I got up and got my orange kimono and headed for the bathroom, I chucked my night kimono on my bed as I walked in and grabbed my sword and headed to the kitchen. Kayato was sitting at the kitchen table eating, Yasumi was eating breakfast, Monikku was sitting next to Kayato, and I sat down in front of a bowl and started eating my breakfast as well.

After I washed up, Kayato and myself went outside we didn't train today we instead did mediation, the time past quickly and Kayato and his family along with Emika went to visit her parents, they were back for two days again. I decided to mediate a bit longer, I haven't mediated for a while, I thought of Jai and Akashi.

When I finally got up from my mediation position I walked back into the house and looked at the time, it was 1:30 pm so I decided to have some lunch. I looked through the fridge to find some rice, I grabbed that and sat down and started eating. After I ate I washed up and headed to the bathroom to clean my teeth, didn't get a chance to clean them this morning.

After this I made my way back to my bedroom to have a lie down. After I had a lie down for a bit I decided to flip through my photo album. I slowly looked through the pages, there was one of myself and Princess Mia at the South Palace and there was one of May-Lyn, Snowbell and me, and there was a photo of Ema and me, and a picture of Diego and me. After I closed the photo album I decided to sit in the lounge room.

I closed my eyes for a bit just inhaling the peace and the tranquillity, just hearing the mini waterfall that is sitting on the mantle peace calmed me down from looking at all those memories. Then I suddenly heard quiet footsteps, I guessed Kayato and his family were back from visiting Emika's family. I suppose it was Monikku playing a trick. I smiled still with my eyes close. The footsteps stopped right at my feet, I was getting a little nervous now because nobody was saying anything. Then I heard this uneven breathing near my ear. My wide smile grew smaller.

"GET UP now quickly get up, why won't you get up; listen get up now or else."

My breathing then became uneven as I tried to recognise that voice but in a second I thought it was Taro joking but something serious sounded in this guy's voice. Then it finally clicked it was Dean. I got up very slowly but Dean slipped his hand underneath my arm and really forced me to stand up. I did not want to open my eyes.

"Open your eyes." I didn't at first and he said it again this time more agitate.

I opened my eyes and looked at him, he grabbed my wrist and pulled me to the front door, and then he pulled me towards the North.

"You have to do what I say, or there will be trouble." Dean informed me.

"What sort of trouble?"

"Keep your mouth shut." He said rudely.

My hand started to shake, he noticed this. "Stop shaking!"

"I can't just stop."

Dean was walking on my left hand side and he positioned his right hand on his hip and then he grabbed my left hand and linked through the gap and held it there. I tried to pull away from him, he grabbed my hand.

"Remember what I said before."

"Okay." I said quietly.

We kept walking to the North markets, and I looked at him.

"Do you mind if I ask a question?" I asked.

"Make it quick."

"Why are you doing this?" I questioned.

"It's all a part of your training, darling." Dean informed me.

"Don't call me darling" I said. "Only one person is allowed to call me darling."

Dean didn't reply, but I looked at him and he smirked.

He pulled me along. I felt sick. After about an hour of walking we finally reached the North markets, we kept walking to the end of the markets. Dean suddenly stopped, I stopped. *What now?* He took his hand in my hand I looked at him; I then looked past him to see Prince Jai. Then all of a sudden Jai looked in my direction but then I got distracted by Dean's head, he moved his head closer I pulled away but with his left hand he put his pointer finger under my chin and he moved his head a bit closer than his lips touched my lips in full lock. I looked towards where Jai was standing and he turned and walked in the other direction. I pulled away from Dean and pushed him, and ran after Jai. I wasn't sure but it sounded like Dean growled. So I stopped in my tracks when I saw Jai get on his horse.

"Jai!" I shouted after him.

He didn't turn around. *Great now he hates me.* I decided to confront Dean about him kissing me. I rushed back to where I had left him.

"Dean" I started to say. "What the hell?"

"Didn't you enjoy that?" He smirked.

"No!" I wanted to hit him but I thought better of it. I leaned toward him and I put my arms around him and I whispered in his ear. "Some training."

His face lit up and said. "I know sweetheart, come on there is more."

I put my hands at my side, then Dean grabbed my right hand and we started walking back to Kayato's house. When I saw Kayato's house we kept walking to the South.

"Um Dean?" I questioned him once again.

"What?"

Gee, what's with him? "Why are we going south?"

"It's all a part of your training"

I didn't say anything after that, as we walked along I thought of Jai and how much he hates me. *Why didn't I just kiss Prince Jai when I had the chance?* We had been walking for ages when we came to the wooden bridge. Dean led me down under the bridge, supporting the wooden bridge was two big wooden beams; Dean led me to nearest one.

"Stay there."

I just stood there looking at him; I put my hands at my sides and wished I didn't. Dean grabbed my hands and placed them behind my back and then he pulled out some rope and tied my hands together.

"Sit down." He demanded.

I sat down. He then moved the rope so it was around my waist and then he walked behind the beam and then came back to face me and then he tied the rope in an army kind of way. Then he smirked at me.

"Try and get out of this one, Anna." He said still smirking. He cut some duct-tape and put across my mouth.

He then walked away, on the way back up on the slant to the main road which we had to walk down to get the beams that held the bridge up, Dean nearly tripped over a stone. I nearly burst out laughing because he was balancing himself like a tight-rope walker. And plus I wouldn't be able to help him because I'm tied up and I'll be laughing so much, but I couldn't laugh because of the duct-tape. I sat there trying to wiggle my hands free, good thing Dean didn't tie my legs together, I moved them to get comfy and moved my body to try to get free but it was no good. I sat there counting in my head, when I got sick of that I tried to guess how long I had been tied up under the bridge, that thought quickly disappeared out of my mind when I heard horses hooves moving along the wooden bridge, just then they stopped. *Creepy, I don't want to know who it was.* Then the footsteps walked along the wooden bridge, I waited. Just then King

Jou came walking down the slant towards me. *Great, just the person I wanted to see.* I was scared because as he walked up to me he pulled out his sword; I had no way to defend myself. *I love you Prince Jai.* I wanted to stand up but I couldn't Dean had tied to rope too tight. King Jou stopped a few feet away from me and stared at me.

"Anna?" He said my name like it was a question.

I wanted to answer him but I couldn't. He walked up to me; he looked at the wooden beam. I watched as he placed his sword between the wooden beam and the rope; he cut the rope with his sword, he kneeled beside me and pulled the rope away, I sat on my knees and pulled myself up that way, I had no other way of getting up, King Jou than cut the rope that held my hands together. I didn't really want to pull the duct-tape off; I was scared that I might pull the skin off my lips. King Jou looked at me.

"Here, I'll do that." He said.

This going to hurt a lot. He lightly put his thumb and pointer finger on the duct-tape and pulled. I wanted to scream. He then stopped.

"Sorry, but this is going to hurt." He said.

He then continued pulling the duct-tape slowly but surely. He removed the duct-tape from across my mouth. I just stood there stunned.

"Anna." King Jou said.

"I uh better go, thanks for saving me." I quietly said and quickly walked away.

"Anna wait." King Jou called after me.

I didn't stop I just wanted to get out of there and back to Kayato's house. Hopefully they were home; as I walked I tried to figure out what was happening with Dean. What had gotten into him lately? I didn't look back at King Jou. *Did Queen Rira tell him about her martial art skill?* Probably not yet, I don't blame her for keeping her skill from him. I looked at the dirt path there was a small stone so I kicked it, I sighed to myself and quickly walked along the dirt path. *How did King Jou know that I was under the bridge? I bet Prince Jai doesn't want to talk to me, I don't blame him, I mean after I told him that I loved him and then he sees Dean and I at the North markets kissing. But I do love Prince Jai.* After the long walk back from the South Bridge I finally made it to Kayato's house.

I walked up the steps and walked straight to the kitchen to have something to eat, I opened the fridge door and began fishing around to see what I could find, there was some rice with pork. Maybe if I just eat the rice and pick the pork out and give it Snowbell, I sat down at the table and began eating the rice, avoiding the pork as best as I could. I chewed slowly to make sure there was no pork, I coughed and nearly spat the rice out yuck some pork got mixed up with the rice. I got the piece of pork out and threw it in the bin; I don't think Snowbell would like to chew a piece of pork that has already been in somebody's mouth. I ate the rest of the rice. At the bottom of the bowl there were nine pieces of pork, there would have been ten if I had looked more carefully. I scooped the pork pieces in my hand and went to find Snowbell, I went to my bedroom first, and she wasn't in there. I walked back to the kitchen, I didn't know if I was allowed in Monikku's room so I thought I'd better not go in there.

"Snowbell?" I called from the kitchen.

Unless Monikku took Snowbell to Emika's parent's house. Just then I heard a whimper, it sounded like it was coming from the lounge, I made my way into the lounge and sure enough Snowbell was curled up near the lounge chair. Her eyes were open. *Ops I must have woken her up.* I sat in the lounge chair; she sat up and stared at me.

"Here Snowbell." I said as I placed one piece of pork in my left hand and kept the other eight in my right hand, I lowered my left hand. I placed the piece of pork between my thumb and pointer finger. Snowbell sniffed it and then she took the piece of pork from my hand. I gave her the other eight pieces.

I then walked along the hallway to the bathroom to wash my hands; I came back into the kitchen to wash up my lunch dishes. And put them back in the right cupboard. *I wonder where Dean got to.* I looked at the time, it was only 6:15 pm. I walked out on the back veranda and sat down and thought of Akashi, after I got bored of sitting down I went to the stables to check on my horse, he had plenty of room to move about in the stables. I patted his blazer. I decided to brush him, his beautiful chocolate brown and white hair; after I brushed him I made sure he had enough water and hay. I walked slowly back up to the house and to the bathroom to wash my hands again. I decided to have a lie down for bit, I walked along the hallway and kept walking to the first bedroom door and lied down on my bed and fell asleep.

I woke up, and went to the kitchen to check the time. *Surely Kayato and his family along with Emika would be back by now.* As I walked into the kitchen I looked at the time and my mouth nearly dropped open, it was

7:15 pm, the house was quiet so that means Kayato and the rest of his family weren't home yet. I decided to go and have a shower; on my way to the bathroom I grabbed my night kimono. I made my way back to my bedroom to put orange kimono in the laundry basket I went back to the bathroom to clean my teeth.

After I came out of the bathroom I decided to take a walk to the South Palace to see Prince Jai, I walked to the front door and down the steps and started to head South on the way there I decided to visit the South Beach, as I walked along I thought of May-Lyn, Jiro and Ema. I made my way down to the South Beach; the tide was slowly coming up to the sand. I made my way down to the sand and I looked to my left and saw Prince Jai, but he had his back to me, I kept looking and I saw another woman with Prince Jai, the way she dressed I could tell she was a Princess. *May-Lyn?* No it wasn't May-Lyn. They were holding hands; I couldn't believe what I saw next. Prince Jai kissed the other woman. My mouth dropped open, I tried to close it but it felt like it had cement holding it down. I stood there stunned thinking what is going on? I then turned my back. I started to cry, I got to the top of the sand to go on the dirt road. I then turned back just as I did Jai looked in my direction then he turned away with the other girl, I walked quickly back to Kayato's house. *So much for Prince Jai loving me.* Ugh I was so angry, not at Prince Jai at myself. I wiped the tears away and kept walking. As I made my way up the front steps to Kayato's house, I went straight to bed I didn't bother to check the time.

I woke up the next morning to find the kitchen empty, I went to the fridge and got some breakfast, I waited just in case they were home before I started to eat, I waited for a bit then started to eat my breakfast, I washed up then went to my bedroom and grabbed my purple kimono and headed to the bathroom to get changed and clean my teeth. On my way pass my bedroom I chucked my night kimono on my bed. And walked onto the back veranda and down the steps'and I walked and sat down and got into a mediation position. *I wonder was King Jou about to tell me about Prince Jai being in a relationship when he rescued me from under the bridge. Why didn't I listen to him?*

I got up from my mediation position and walked to the stables and saddled my horse and I took off towards my Grandparents. I took my time; I wanted to look at the trees, just Mother Nature doing her job. As my horse trotted towards the front veranda of their house; Genichi came down the steps to greet me.

"Morning Anna."

"Morning Genichi." I answered him.

I walked up the front steps and walked in the kitchen, Diego came bounding out from under the table, and he looked at me and barked as if to say "Hello Anna."

"Hey Diego." I said and patted his big grey body.

Just then Grandma came out of the lounge room. "Diego I was—" She began to say until she saw me standing there.

"Anna." Her voice said happily.

"Hey Grandma."

She walked towards me and lightly grabbed my hand and pulled me towards the lounge she might be elderly but she still has strength, their lounge room was slightly more bigger than Kayato's, in the top left hand corner the window had sun coming through the curtain, they were white. In the bottom left hand corner was the lounge chair. We sat down; Grandma's hazel eyes looked into mine.

"What's wrong, Anna? She suddenly said.

I nearly burst out crying. "I told Prince Jai that I love him, but just recently Dean and I were at the North markets and I saw Jai there, then Dean kissed me, Jai saw this" I paused to catch my breath then continued. "Jai walked away, so I pushed Dean away and went after Jai, by the time I caught up to Jai he was already on his horse." I stopped to take another breather.

"Anna, what else happened?"

"And then last night I went to the South beach before I went to the South palace, at the beach I saw Jai there but he was with another woman, and then they kissed each other" I paused. "I then walked away back to the dirt road and then I turned around and Jai turned around too, he saw me but then he walked away with the other woman." I said with tears in my eyes.

She put her arm around me and squeezed me. I just sat there wiping the tears away. I thought of my parents. We sat in silence for a bit, just then we heard footsteps, Diego ears went straight up he was also listening. I smiled.

"Marree." It was Grandpa's voice.

"In the lounge Jeff." She answered'back.

Grandpa and Akashi came into the lounge. They were surprised to see me.

"Anna." Akashi and Grandpa said at the same time.

"Hey." I said. I then stood up and walked up to Akashi.

"Let's go outside." I said to him.

"Okay."

Akashi and I walked back to the kitchen and walked out the side door and we sat down on the steps. Akashi is like an older brother to me, I can almost tell him anything. We sat in silence.

"How's your training going? Akashi suddenly said.

"It's going good, a part from Kayato not being home at the moment."

"Oh."

I smiled. But I guess Akashi could see the sadness in my eyes.

"Are you okay? He asked.

"No, I'm not okay."

"Do you want to talk about it?

"Yeah."

He sat there waiting for me to tell him, good thing Akashi is patient.

"Long story short" I started. "I told Jai that I love him, and then recently Dean and I were at the North markets, Jai was there. Dean kissed me, Jai saw this and walked away, I went after Jai but he had already got on his horse" I paused. "Last night I went to the South beach and Jai was there with another woman and he kissed her, I walked back up to the main road and I turned around and Jai looked at me and then he walked away with the other girl." I finally said and saw Akashi's face.

"He did what?!" Akashi nearly shouted. He stood up and practically jumped down the steps.

"Where is he, I'm going to teach him how to respect women." He said as he walked away.

I quickly got up and ran after him, I caught up to him and with both hands grabbed his left upper arm and tried to pull him back towards my Grandparents house, but he was too strong as he walked I got pulled along.

"Akashi, please don't." I said.

"He hurt you and no one hurts you." Akashi said.

"Akashi, I know you're angry but please don't hurt Jai."

"And why shouldn't I? He deserves it." Akashi shot back.

"No Akashi, no one deserves to get hurt, but people do, it's a way of life." I said hoping that would make sense.

Then all of sudden he stopped walking; I nearly smashed into the back of him. *Ops I should have kept my mouth shut.* I let go of his arm and he turned around. He put his arms around me he leaned in and said "I know that you look up to me as a brother, but at the moment I just want to hold you."

I nodded and said "Okay."

He held me in his arms. He looked at me. "I want to make sure that you are safe and I know that I might regret this later, but I want to kiss you" He paused. "Is that Okay?"

I smiled and nodded and said "Yeah."

Akashi put his hands lightly on my lower back and I stretched my arms up and placed them around the back of his neck. I closed my eyes and so did Akashi. We automatically leaned in towards each other and our lips touched together and I moved my lips with his, we kissed for a bit. Akashi then stopped, I opened my eyes, he then put his pointer finger under my chin and moved my chin towards him and we kissed again but shorter this time. *Wow.* I looked at him, he smiled and I smiled back at him. I turned around and started walking back to my grandparents' house.

"Anna." Akashi said and he placed his hand on my shoulder.

"I'm sorry Akashi, but I only think of you as a brother to me. I hope this doesn't change anything about us." I said to him.

"It won't."

Akashi put his arm around my back and we walked back to my grandparent's house. As we made our way back towards my grandparents, I thought about staying the whole day there. I should have brought Snowbell as well; she hasn't seen Diego in a while.

I flashed back to when May-Lyn and I first brought Snowbell to my grandparents house and she saw Diego, her little white tail went between her legs and her ears went back her on her head and she whimpered. May-Lyn and I were standing in the kitchen and Snowbell was standing at May-Lyn's feet. Diego just stared at her and then he walked up to her and sniffed her. Snowbell growled at Diego as if to tell him to stay away. Diego then sat down and Snowbell bounded towards Diego and kind of tugged on his hair he then got up and Snowbell bolted towards the front door and shot down the steps Diego chased after her. So May-Lyn and I went after the dogs, Diego had a stick in his mouth and as May-Lyn and I finally caught up to them Diego dropped the stick, May-Lyn picked up the stick and threw it and Diego chased after it, so did Snowbell.

"Anna." Akashi's voice pulled me back to reality.

We were walking towards the front veranda of my grandparent's house.

"Yes Akashi?" I answered.

"How long are you going to be here today?"

"Most of the day, I'll head back to Kayato's house at four." I informed Akashi.

Akashi smiled. "Good." He said and pulled me closer to him.

Akashi and I walked up the steps and into the kitchen to find Grandma and Grandpa having morning tea. I got two cups and made Akashi and I a cup of tea, I brought the cups of tea out to the kitchen table Akashi sat down, and I sat down beside him. I didn't feel like eating anything so I slowly drank my tea. The time at my grandparents house went quickly, Akashi went with Grandpa to help him muck out the stables, I could of went along but I didn't feel really up to it. Instead Grandma and I sat in the lounge looking through some of the photo albums, the photo album we were looking through the cover of it was red with gold writing, and it reminded me of Prince Jai's red and gold kimono. The writing on the photo album said "*Photos are memories of the Past and Present.*" There was this one photo of us when we were still in Australia, our house was a beautiful Queenslander home with the veranda that reached all around the house, the house was painted white and the rails of the veranda were painted dark blue. We use to live on a cattle property which was thirty kilometres away from the nearest town. In the evening my parents and I would watch the sun set. My parents would sit really close to each other on the top step and I would sit on my Mum or Dad's lap, which ever I felt like sitting on.

"I miss Australia." I suddenly said.

"I do too sweetheart." Grandma said.

I looked at another photo; this photo was of me and a little potty calf. I named the potty calf Splotches, he was white with black splotches, I had my little cowgirl hat on and jeans and a long sleeved shirt. Even though I was three at the time when I named him I had trouble saying his name so I just said Splot and one time I even said Spot. But my parents knew what I meant, that was the main thing.

"Oh, I remember that." Grandma looked at the photo.

I smiled at the photo. "Yeah." I replied.

She was the one who took the photo.

I flashed back to when Dad decided to move back to Japan, it was a month after my fourth birthday. I was in bed trying to get to sleep when I heard Dad talking to Mum. They were both in the kitchen which was right near my bedroom, when they would talk after I had gone to bed I would try to listen to what they would talk about, I had my teddy bear with me.

"Lisa." Dad's voice said.

"David." Mum's voice answered him.

I heard him pull the chair out from the table and he sat down.

"I'm thinking about moving back to Japan" Dad said to her. "And I want you and Anna to come with me."

Mum went quiet for a bit; I lied awake waiting for her to answer.

"Can I think about it?" She finally said.

"Sure." Dad said.

She got up and started to come into my bedroom, I quickly shut my eyes. She sat down on my bed and stroked my hair.

"My baby girl is growing up." She said.

I just kept my eyes closed; she leant down and kissed my cheek.

I snapped back to reality, and looked at some more photos. After a bit Akashi and Grandpa came back inside, I checked the time, it was nearly 4:00 pm. Grandma and Grandpa along with Akashi walked to the front veranda with me, I said goodbye to my Grandparents and Akashi decided to escort me back to Kayato's place. Akashi was on the right side of me. Along the dirt path Akashi didn't say anything so I decided to start the conversation:

"How has work been lately?"

"Oh yeah good, not as busy as we were last week. We had about thirty orders to fill last week"

"How many this week?"

"Ten."

"Awesome."

He smiled, and we kept going along the dirt path.

"Where's Dean lately?" Akashi asked.

"I haven't got clue where he is."

"Oh."

I smiled and Akashi smiled back, I just could see Kayato's house roof coming into view when I noticed Akashi stopped smiling. I looked straight ahead, and who should be coming along the dirt path? But Prince Jai.

"Akashi don't." I said quietly.

"I'm not going to do anything." He replied.

As we past Prince Jai on his grey horse with his red and gold kimono on, and two south officers, I nearly fainted when I looked at Akashi. He was looking at Jai in a way that I wouldn't even think was humanly possible. As Prince Jai and the officers passed us; Akashi made his eyes follow Jai. As we got further away from them I looked at Akashi, his face was calmer.

"Akashi!" I said.

"What?" He had a cheeky smile on his face.

"Why did you go and do that for?"

He shrugged his shoulders "Because I felt like it."

While we rode along the dirt path we didn't talk much, then we came to Kayato's house. I said bye to Akashi and he turned his horse around and went back the way we'd come to head home. I took my horse to the stables unsaddled him, I then washed him, and then brushed him. He had no water so I went around the side of stables and found a tap. I took his water bucket out and filled it, there was only so much water I could put in without being unable to carry it. I took it back to the stables and put it back where it had come from. Hopefully he won't drink all that within an hour. He had enough hay, so I walked back up to the house to wash my hands and to have a rest. I quickly made my way up the back steps of the wooden veranda and dashed into the kitchen, past my bedroom and into the bathroom to wash my hands, and also to clean my teeth. *It has been a day since Kayato's family along with Emika went to visit her parents*

I came to the door way of my bedroom to find Dean sitting on my bed, I noticed he had my locket in his hand it was open and he was looking at the picture it held of my parents. He looked at me, but he didn't move his head.

"Your parents were so easy to kill." He said smirking.

"Excuse me?" I said shocked.

He threw the locket down on the bed and got up and pulled out his sword, I made a run for it; I rushed for the front door. I jumped down the steps and headed north no way was I going south. As I ran a hira-shuriken hit the tree on my left. I ran a bit faster, I couldn't keep running forever, sooner or later I would have to stop. Then I saw some bushes up ahead, I made my way to the bushes and ducked down, I put my hand over my mouth to stop the sound of my panting. Just then I heard footsteps. But they were in a different direction, I turned my body around to see if I could see Dean, nope so sign of him, I quietly got up and started to run again, until my foot snapped on a branch. *GREAT! That's all I need.* I was about to run again until:

"Anna." Dean's voice said from behind me.

I turned around. "Why are you doing this? You're meant to be my mentor." I asked him.

"Because I have to." He said still smirking.

"Please Dean, what do you want from me?" I asked.

"I don't want anything from you."

"Why did you have to kill my parents?!" I shouted at Dean.

"As I said before I had to."

"How could you do any of this?!" I managed to say. "And you promised Princess Mia that you would look after me."

"That bit was true." He stated.

"What so now you're just going to kill me?"

"Yes." He smirked.

I was angry now, I took out my sword. He took out his sword and rushed at me, I blocked his move, I aimed for his arm but that was no good he knocked my sword out of the way, I took a step back and ran.

"Not again." I heard Dean say behind me.

I had no idea what I was going to do once I stopped running, I felt sick. I trusted Dean, my entire family trusted him. King Jou trusted him, Kayato trusted him as well. I stopped running and turned around to face Dean. He came to a stop as well.

"My entire family trusted you!" I shouted at him.

"So?" He said bluntly.

And then it came to me, he had this planned out from the beginning. Once I got close to Prince Jai, he would destroy our relationship by making Jai see us kissing.

"You set me up!" I said.

"My sweet Anna, you finally put all the pieces together" He said. "Once I assassinated your parents, I asked King Jou if you could work for him, he said yes straight away. But then you were forming a relationship with his son. I had no choice but to get you away from the South Palace—"

I interrupted him:

"It was you! You told King Jou that I didn't have permission to speak with Prince Jai."

"I had no other choice and I knew that you wouldn't accept his duel."

"You make me sick!"

He smiled at this. "That Thursday morning when Jai came to visit you, I was meant to finish you off then, but he got there before me, so I decided to break into your bedroom window to finish the job, but when I threw the knife Kayato blocked it with his sword." He said calmly.

"Does King Jou know about any of this?" I asked.

"No."

I just stood there looking at him, then I thought of Kayato and his family along with Emika and her parents. "Why didn't you just finish me off when we were coming to Kayato's house?" I asked.

"I couldn't be bothered." He said.

"What did you say to Prince Jai?" I asked him. Wanting to know what was going on.

"I didn't tell him anything."

"What did you do Kayato and his family and Emika's?"

He chuckled, it was kind of scary. "Why, I just let their horses roam free."

"What else?" I demanded.

"They're fine, but the question is; are you going to be?"

I glared at him. And again I took out my sword, he pulled out his sword, I rushed at him this time I tried to aim for his thigh, I just nicked it. He looked at the wound, I took a step back.

"You'll pay for that, you little brat." He growled.

"Who you calling little?"

I smiled. Then he rushed at me, he had his sword straight out in front of him, I blocked it but just barely. *He trained with Kayato and me to find out my weak points!* I forced him to walk backwards as we duelled. I aimed for his hand, he blocked the strike and he kept walking backwards and I moved forwards. Forcing him back to Kayato's house, I hoped Dean wouldn't figure this out. He swung the sword around his head and aimed at me; I ducked and shouldered him in the stomach.

"Ugh!" He said through barred teeth.

"Ops, sorry did I hurt you" I smirked.

He glared at me; he threw his sword to the right side of him. *What the heck?* He then stood in fighting stance. I quickly realised what he was doing; I quickly put my sword back in its scabbed, if I threw it on the ground Dean would probably pick it up and use it against me. I turned and ran, I heard Dean growl. As I ran further up the dirt path I saw King Daichi and six of the North guards rushing towards me, the guards were behind King Daichi in a straight line. I stopped and turned around to find Dean on the right hand side of path out from behind a tree came his horse; he climbed on and took off. I turned back around to face King Daichi, he and the six guards were just getting to me.

"After him." King Daichi said to the six guards.

"Yes Your Highness." All the guards said at once, it kind of sounded like the one guard was repeating himself five times.

The guards went after Dean, good thing the guards were on horses, I peered around King Daichi to find another six guards; King Daichi's grey horse took a step forward I froze.

"Easy boy." King Daichi said and patted his horses' neck. "Anna."

I stopped looking at the guards and turned my attention to King Daichi.

"Yes Your Highness."

"Did Dean hurt you?" He asked.

"No."

"Good." He said bluntly.

Just then one of the six guards behind King Daichi rode towards me but when he got to King Daichi side he suddenly stopped. I noticed the guard had another horse with him.

"I want you to come to the North Palace." King Daichi said.

"Okay."

I climbed on the spare horse, and we set off towards the North Palace. As we rode along I thought of Snowbell.

"Um Your Highness." I said kind of nervous.

"Yes Anna."

"What about Snowbell?"

"Takahiro go back to Kayato's house and find Snowbell." King Daichi said as he turned his face to tell the guard.

"Yes Your Highness." Takahiro said.

As we went along to the North Palace I thought of Jai. *If only I could see Prince Jai and explain everything, that Dean kissed me, I didn't kiss Dean. But I guess what difference will it make now, Jai already has got somebody else.* I sighed to myself. *Jai probably thinks that I lied to him about loving him.* I stopped that thought and concentrated on the dirt path. I thought of Ema and what she would be doing. Probably at May-Lyn's. We kept going along the path and up a head I could see the North markets, not very far now to the North Palace.

We stopped several feet away from the North Markets to get off our horses. Through the markets we had to walk on foot and lead our horses. I took my time, I didn't rush, and I didn't want to spook my horse. As we waited for the last guard to get through the crowd of people the rest of us were already on our horses, the last guard then climbed back on his horse and we set off towards the palace. As we arrived at the North palace we rode our horses just outside the stables. The stable hands went straight to their work unsaddling, getting fresh water and feed for the horses. We then entered the palace it was huge there was a large room on the walls it was well lit with portraits of Kings and Queens who ruled before King Daichi and Queen Miranda. There was a stairwell several feet away from where King Daichi and I were standing leading up to other rooms. A servant came down the stairs she could not have been anymore older then I am, she had brown hair and soft brown eyes, soot on her face in fact she had sot all over her and her clothes were a mess not that she was wearing very little it was almost like a sheet with holes for arms, legs and her head.

"Follow me."

I looked at King Daichi for reassurance, he nodded.

"Dinner will be at six o'clock sharp, see you there." King Daichi said.

I walked up the stairs after the servant, and as I reached my room the servant turned to me.

"There are clean towels, and sheets on your bed and the soap is in the bathroom. The bathroom is the last door on your right. If you have any questions please feel free to ask me."

"I do have a question, well two actually."

She looked at me.

I asked her what her name is and I told her what my name is.

"Jasmine. But Jazz for short." She replied.

"Cool, why do you wear those clothes for?"

"Long story short, we're so many years behind the South, East and West Palaces, that's why I have to wear these, King Daichi is trying to get it changed" Jazz paused "And I'll be out of a job soon, well at least as a servant anyway."

"I am so sorry." I said.

"It's okay." Jazz said.

The bed was a queen sized which was in the middle of the room and the bed head against the wall, no curtains around it though, it didn't worry me. On the left hand side there was a duchess with a mirror. On the right hand side there was an arch window, and at the back wall was a wardrobe. I then thought what I am going to do for clothes.

"Jasmine?" I asked.

"Yes Anna?" Jazz asked.

"I was just wondering what I'm going to do for clothes." I answered her.

"Come with me."

I stood up and walked towards the door, Jazz shut it behind her.

"Princess May-Lyn should have some kimonos that she has grown out of that might fit you" Jazz said.

And she started walking along the hallway, I followed her, as we walked along I took notice that the Palace was very plain inside. We kept walking and then we came to a halt. We were at a wooden door with a gold handle; the other doorknobs were all silver. *Oh I get it, the gold symbolizes which is the royalties bedrooms and the silver means that there the guest rooms.* Jasmine opened the door and we walked in. I looked around the room, May-Lyn's bedroom had a queen sized bed with curtains, the back wall had a huge duchess and the left hand side had a wardrobe, and in the corner there was a standing mirror, on the right hand side there was another arch window. Jasmine walked up to the wardrobe and opened it. I watched as she pulled out four kimonos. One was yellow with white flowers, the second was blue with white, the third was white and around the sleeves and collar of the arms and neck were black, and the fourth was black and had white around the arm sleeves and collar. Jasmine handed me the first one and walked out of the room. *Jasmine, I don't want to get caught in May-Lyn's bedroom.* I wanted to say, but too late she had already walked out the door and closed it.

I tried the first kimono on, it fitted nicely. I then put my purple kimono back on. I quietly walked to the door and opened it to find Jasmine had her back to the door.

"Jazz." I said.

She spun around to face me.

"It fits." I told her.

Jasmine smiled and took the kimono from me and handed me the second one.

"Thanks."

I then closed the door and tried the blue and white kimono on, it was a bit tight, and it felt like I couldn't breathe properly. I quickly took it off and put my purple kimono on. And opened the door and handed Jazz it.

"This one is too tight."

"Okay."

She handed me the third one and I shut the door, I quickly got changed and the third one fitted. I opened the door.

"Jazz the third one fits"

"Cool."

She then handed me the fourth one, I quickly shut the door and tried it on, and it fitted. I was hoping it would. I got changed, then opened the door and walked out.

"This one fits also." I informed Jazz.

"Cool, I'll just put the blue and white one back." Jazz said.

She handed me the other three kimonos and opened May-Lyn's bedroom door and walked in with the blue and white kimono. Just as Jazz closed the door behind her, the sound of people's voice's started to come towards us. I put the kimonos behind my back. *Why on earth did I just do that for, that doesn't me look suppositious at all.* The voices got closer, just then Jazz came out of May-Lyn's bedroom,

I sighed a breath of relief. I put the kimonos back in front of me.

"Here I'll take those."

I handed Jazz the three kimonos, just then the voices and the footsteps stopped. I gulped.

"Anna!" May-Lyn shouted, her voice echoed through the palace.

She and Ema rushed towards Jazz and me. When May-Lyn hasn't seen in someone ages that she cares about, I thought that she would stop a few feet away from them before she hugs them. But not today she kept rushing towards me, Ema stopped and I guess she knew what was about to happen. May-Lyn tried to stop but she couldn't, she crushed into me, I went flying on the floor and May-Lyn landed next me, but she was in position like she was ready to do push-ups, her hair hung loosely around her head, I couldn't really see her face.

"Good to see you May."

She then sat down cross-legged. "Ops, sorry I didn't mean to knock you over." She said.

"It's okay."

We quickly got up off the floor; May-Lyn looked at Jasmine.

"Anna doesn't have any clothes with her, so I said that she could borrow some of your kimonos, I hope that is okay with you, Your Highness." Jasmine said when May-Lyn looked her.

"Yes of course it's okay with me Jasmine, you don't have to ask." May-Lyn answered with a smile.

Jasmine smiled. "I'll put these on your bed, Anna."

"Okay."

After Jasmine went down the hallway we followed her and we walked down the steps and turned left, May-Lyn led Ema and me to a door that was big and wooden and it was arch, May-Lyn opened the door and we all walked in. My mouth nearly dropped open, in the middle of the room was a huge table with candles between plates of food. King Daichi was sitting at the head of the table, his wife Queen Miranda was sitting on the left hand side of him. May-Lyn sat facing her mother, Ema sat down next to May-Lyn and I sat down next to Ema. In front of us there was rice and pork. *Oh there's pork in mine. I looked at Ema's, she had no pork. I wanted to swap with her, but I thought I better not say anything.* I decided to eat the pork; I will get a headache from it later but oh well. We were just about to eat our meal when the doors burst opened.

"You're Highness." It was Takahiro's voice.

"Yes?" King Daichi asked.

"I have Snowbell and Anna's locket." Takahiro answered.

Even though I had my back to Takahiro, I noticed that King Daichi looked more closely at him.

"What happened to your finger Takahiro?" King Daichi asked.

"Snowbell bit me when I tried to pick her up and then ran off, that's why it took me so long to get back." Takahiro answered King Daichi.

"Where was she when you found her?" King Daichi shot back.

"She was hiding under Anna's bed, Your Highness."

King Daichi focused his attention on me. "Anna."

I looked at King Daichi. "Yes Your Highness?'

"Do you want your locket now?" He asked.

"No." I answered him bluntly.

King Daichi nodded and then focused back Takahiro. "Please take Anna's locket to the guest room where she is staying."

"Yes Your Highness."

I could see out of the corner of my eye Takahiro turned around and bobbed down and stood back up and faced us; in his hands were Snowbell. He then put her back down and walked away and closed the door behind him. Snowbell barked. King Daichi grabbed another spare plate and put some pork on it and put it on the floor, Snowbell walked up to it, she sniffed it and then started eating. I didn't really want to eat the pork but I forced myself to. It was after dinner when the doors burst opened again.

"You're Highness." The guard said breathlessly.

"Yes A.J?" King Daichi said as he poured the guard a drink of water.

"We couldn't catch Dean, he headed east."

King Daichi handed A.J the glass of water, A.J took the glass of water from King Daichi.

"Thank you, Your Highness."

"I'll ride over to the East tomorrow and inform the officers of what is happening."

A.J finished drinking his glass of water and headed out the door.

After dinner I went back the guest bedroom to find the locket placed on the duchess, I grabbed the black and white kimono and headed to the bathroom to a have shower, I carried my folded purple kimono in both hands, I didn't want to drop it just in case King Daichi or Queen Miranda were looking for me. I opened the door of the guestroom and walked in and put my purple kimono along with the other three kimonos in the wardrobe and sat down on the bed. The headache was about to set in. Just then there was knocking at the door.

"Come in." I said softly.

The door opened and there stood May-Lyn, in her hand was a tooth brush.

"I thought you might want this, it's a spare, and it hasn't been used."

She walked up to the bed and sat down next to me, I took the brush from her hand.

"Thanks" I started to say. "I might clean my teeth and go to bed."

"Yeah it's been a pretty full on day."

I nodded. "And also I have a headache."

"Did your rice have pork in it?" She asked.

"Yes." I said lightly.

"You could've said something."

"Honestly May-Lyn it's okay."

"Are you sure?"

"Yes, I could do with a goodnights sleep."

"Okay" She said as she hugged me. "Goodnight Anna."

"Goodnight May-Lyn."

She then got up and walked out but left the door open, I got up and walked to the bathroom to clean my teeth, I just left the tooth brush in the bathroom, I quickly made my way from the bathroom to the guest bedroom, pulled back the cover got in and got comfy, tonight I didn't think of Jai. I fell asleep quickly.

That night I dreamt of Jai and that woman he kissed at the beach, I was standing there watching them. I woke up with a fright; I rolled over onto my left side and sighed, I tried to go back to sleep.

I woke up next morning, I wasn't sure if I was to go straight to breakfast or get changed, I decided to get changed, I grabbed the yellow kimono and quietly slipped off to the bathroom. After I came out of the bathroom I went back to the guest bedroom to put the black and white kimono back on the bed and went down stairs to the dining room. As I made my way down the stairs I took my time, as I came down the last step I quickly walked to the door.

Chapter 10

The Surprise

I was about to open the door to the dining room when May-Lyn called out to me.

"Anna."

I turned around to face her, with her she had Ema they quickly walked towards me.

"Morning Anna." Ema said.

"Morning."

Snowbell came bounding up behind them, and bumped into the back of Ema's legs, Ema looked behind her and a smile spread across her face. May-Lyn opened the door and we all walked in including Snowbell. I wasn't really paying much attention to who was sitting at the table; I was looking at the wall and thinking of Akashi.

"Anna!" A voice said.

This made me look at the table, I found Monikku sitting in between her parents, Kayato was sitting of the left side of his daughter and Yasumi was sitting on her right side.

"Hey." I answered her.

I took a glance down the table to find Taro who was sitting next to Kayato and Emika was sitting beside him. I was glad to see that they were okay and Dean didn't hurt them, I noticed that Queen Miranda was sitting where May-Lyn sat last night while we ate dinner, May-Lyn sat beside her mother, Ema sat next to her and I sat next to Ema, Snowbell flopped down on the floor. Just then King Daichi walked into the room, he walked to Queen Miranda's chair put his left arm around her back and leant'his head down to kiss her, I didn't watch after his lips moved closer, I looked at the bowl that was in front of me.

"Please parents, keep it PG, we have kids here." May-Lyn piped up.

King Daichi didn't say anything, and I guessed he was still kissing his wife.

"I'll be back this afternoon." King Daichi suddenly said.

"Okay, love you." Queen Miranda's voice said.

"Love you too, see you May."

She didn't look at her father; she was too busy looking at her bowl. "Bye, love you."

Love you too May." King Daichi said and headed out the door.

I noticed Kayato staring at me from the other side of the table; I decided to not make eye contact with him unless I really have to. I felt sick, I didn't want to eat breakfast, I just want to run out that door and keep going until I get to the front entrance and then keep running, it would be as simple as counting to three. But life isn't simple, parents don't tell their children that and why should they, we're just going to find out sooner or later. And for me it was later in life I found out that life wasn't fair, I had a happy life when we were living in Australia, sure it was only four years of my life but it was the best time of my young life. While we were living in Australia on our cattle property, my parents become friendly with the next door neighbours, they only lived down the road which was pretty good. They were the Anderson family, they had a son about my age when we left to go and live in Japan. Their son was named Brody. They also owned a cattle property. I smiled a little smile as I remembered what Brody looked like; he had darkish blonde hair and hazel eyes. Brody and I use to go to Kindergarten together that was the good old days.

Now days my life is full of sadness, anger, betrayal by people I trusted or thought I could trust. Kayato was still staring at me; I don't think he had blinked once since I sat down. *I think I just figured it out why he is looking at me. He probably thinks that I had something do with Dean setting their horses free. That's just great now, thanks a lot Dean. Not!* As we started to eat breakfast, I felt sicker. I quickly ate my breakfast. May-Lyn and Ema finished just after me, we then went out of the room, I was thankful for that, Snowbell didn't follow she had fallen asleep. May-Lyn led us out to the courtyard which was behind the palace not at the front like most courtyards were.

As we walked into the courtyard it was fairly huge, but then why wouldn't it be. In the middle there was a white arch and surrounding the arch was this beautiful garden with flowers that came around the arch like a love heart, at the bottom it was separated but at the top was joined, there was also a cherry tree in the left corner; there was some distance between the arch and the cherry tree, and the palace walls which were made out of limestone which were a creamy colour and then there is the green grass which just makes the courtyard look like something out of a fairytale.

"My parents got married in this garden." May-Lyn informed Ema and me.

Ema looked around and then focused back on May-Lyn. "Wow." Ema said in amazament.

"I know." May-Lyn said with a smile on her face.

"It's so beautiful." I said.

"Yep." May-Lyn answered, with the smile still on her face.

"I need to clean my teeth." Ema burst out.

"Me too." May-Lyn said.

"Me three." I said.

All three of us started walking back into the palace, we walked around the side, and then up to the front entrance of the palace we walked up the stairs and kept going until we got to the bathroom, Ema went first, I rested my back against the wall, May-Lyn stood next to me.

"Thanks for all this." I said quietly I wasn't sure if she had heard what I said. I kept looking at the floor.

"It's okay." She said when she turned her face towards me.

Just then Ema came out of the bathroom; May-Lyn went in next. Ema stood where May-Lyn had.

"Are you okay?" Ema said.

"Yep." I answered and smiled at her.

May-Lyn came out a couple minutes later, I went into the bathroom. I found my tooth brush where I had left it last night. I quickly cleaned my teeth and walked out to where May-Lyn and Ema were.

"What do you want to do now?" May-Lyn asked us.

"Can we go back outside?" Ema asked.

"Sure."

All three of us went back outside, and we sat on the garden seat. May-Lyn and Ema talked, I just listened to their conversation.

"Are you staying again tonight, Ema?" May-Lyn asked.

Ema was about to answer her when one of the guards came walking towards us. He stopped just a few feet away from May-Lyn. This guard was tall, with black hair and chocolate brown eyes. I kept staring at him.

"Sorry to interrupt Your Highness, but Kayato would like to speak to Anna."

"It's okay, Takahiro."

Takahiro nodded and looked at me; I stood up and walked towards Takahiro. We walked side by side, we went around the side and up to the front entrance, Takahiro opened the door for us and we walked in and Takahiro turned right which took us to a wooden door. *Why does Kayato want to talk to me?* Takahiro opened the door for me, inside the room on the left hand side was two bookshelves backed up against the side wall, a desk and a chair and photo of King Daichi, Queen Miranda and May-Lyn, there was nobody in the room expect me.

"Kayato will be along in a minute." Takahiro informed me.

"Okay." I managed to say.

He closed the door behind him and I heard his footsteps walk away, I decided to stand opposite side of the bookshelves, and I rested my back against the wall and looked at the bookshelves. I could hear footsteps, and by the sounds of it there were two people, I turned my head and watched the door opening, and the door revealed who was standing on the other side, it was Takahiro and Kayato, and Kayato wore a white kimono with blue around the collar and arm sleeves.

"Thank you Takahiro." Kayato said.

"It's okay Kayato." Takahiro answered Kayato.

Kayato to took a step into the room; Takahiro shut the door behind him and walked off. *Ops I forgot to thank Takahiro for opening the door for me.* Kayato stood, he didn't move. *He wanted to speak to me, so why wasn't he saying anything? Please say something.*

"Please say something." I said after I had thought it.

I turned away from him and stared at the wall. *Anna, keep your mouth closed. I told myself.*

"What do you want me to say? I put my entire family in harm's way." He said harshly.

"What so it's my fault that Dean let your horses go free?"

"No—"

I interrupted him. "When something goes bad I get the blame whether I did it or not."

"Anna, I'm not blaming you, I saw Dean untie our horses" He said. "But how did you know that Dean let them go?"

"He told me." I said. A moment later "Well at least he didn't chase you." I mumbled.

"Excuse me?" Kayato asked.

I turned my head towards Kayato. "I said at least he didn't hurt anyone."

Kayato didn't say anything. I decided that this conversation was done, I started to walk towards the door, and Kayato blocked my way. *Now what?*

"We're not done." Kayato informed me.

"I have nothing more to say."

"Anna, what happened while I was away?"

"What happened? Why don't you ask Prince Jai what happened, he can tell you, and ask Dean when the East guards find him." I answered him.

I found a gap and tried to get past, but Kayato moved his body so I couldn't.

"No, I'm not going to ask Prince Jai what happened, I want you to tell me."

"Okay, I'll tell you what happened only if I can leave the bit about Prince Jai out."

"Okay."

"Well Dean said it was a apart of my training, I can't believe I actually believed what he was telling me, we went to the South bridge Dean tied me up, and put duct-tape on my mouth and left me there, not long after he had left, King Jou came under the bridge and saved me. And then yesterday Dean told me what he had done—"

Kayato interrupted me. "What do you mean by what he had done?" His face looked angry.

"He told me that my parents were so easy to kill, and then I ran from him and he chased me. So I hid in some bushes so I could catch my breath and then I was about to run again when my foot snapped on a branch, he was behind me and he said my name and I turned to face him to confront him about why he was doing this, and he told me and so we fought for a bit, I injured him in the thigh, but he escaped on his horse when King Daichi was heading our way."

"Your safe now, that's what matters." Kayato said gently.

"I guess." I said quietly.

"What else happened?"

"I don't want to talk about it."

"Anna—"

I cut in. "I said I don't want to talk about it."

I moved past him, and this time he didn't try to stop me. I opened the door and closed it behind me, I then made my way to the stairs and ran up them and went to the guest bedroom opened the door and quickly closed it behind me and made my way to the bed, I got to where the pillow was and my knees buckled under me, I put my arms on the pillow and rested my head on my right arm. I flashed back to where I was at the South beach and Prince Jai was there with that other woman. After the flash back, I climbed back on to the bed with my arms and head still in the position. *May-Lyn and Ema would be looking for me.* I lied on the bed a bit longer, I thought of Akashi. Just then footsteps came bounding towards my door, it swung open.

"I told you we find her here." May-Lyn looked at Ema.

"Yes detective." Ema answered her with a cheeky smile.

"We thought you got lost." May-Lyn said looking at me.

"It's easy enough to do." Ema said trying to cheer me up.

I sat up looking at them, they both sat down on the bed. May-Lyn sat on my right side and Ema sat on my left. I sat there and said nothing. So we sat in silence for a bit.

"Anna?"

All three of us looked towards the door, standing there was Monikku with her brown eyes peering into the room with her she had a guard.

"Come here sweetheart." May-Lyn said.

Monikku turned to the guard. "Bye mister guard."

"Anytime Monikku." The guard said.

She then turned and walked into the room, the guard went. Monikku walked up to May-Lyn, and she lifted Monikku onto her lap, Monikku sat with her little legs across May-Lyn's thighs and was facing me. I smiled at her, she smiled back.

"Can I see the horses please?" Monikku looked at May-Lyn.

"You sure can."

Monikku climbed off May-Lyn's lap and took a step forward, spun around to face May-Lyn. I stood up and so did Ema, I grabbed my locket from the duchess. Monikku grabbed May-Lyn's hand and Ema's hand I walked next to Ema, we went out the door, I closed it. And we walked down the stairs, between the stairs and the entrance May-Lyn and Ema were lifting Monikku up off the floor.

"One, two, three, and jump" May-Lyn and Ema said.

As we made our way outside, an idea came to me. As we walked near the stables I saw my horse.

"May-Lyn." I said.

"Yes Anna?"

"Would it be okay if I go and see Akashi?"

"Of course it is I'll get one of the stable hands to saddle your horse."

As we got closer to the stables, Monikku smiled.

"Akio can you please saddle Anna's horse for her."

He was short with black hair, and his brown eyes twinkled. "Yes Your Highness."

Monikku let go of May-Lyn's and Ema's hands and she tugged on May-Lyn's kimono sleeve. May-Lyn looked down.

"I want to pat the horsey." Monikku said.

May-Lyn smiled and picked up Monikku. "Which one would you like to pat?"

There were about eight horses in the stables.

"That one." Monikku pointed to May-Lyn's grey horse.

May-Lyn who was still carrying Monikku walked over to her horse, May-Lyn put Monikku close enough so she could reach out her little hand and pat the horse's blazer.

"Miss Anna."

I looked over to where Akio was standing. "Yes?"

"Your horse is ready." Akio said as he led him out of the stables.

I put my locket on. "Thank you." I said. I climbed on and turned him around to face May-Lyn, Ema and Monikku.

"I should be back by lunch time."

"Okay." May-Lyn said.

"Bye, bye." Monikku waved.

"Bye, see you soon."

I turned my horse around and headed to Akashi's house, hopefully he was home. I didn't really want to go to the South Palace by myself. It was a short horse ride from the North Palace to Akashi's, when I got to Akashi's I got off my horse and went up to the front door and knocked. I waited for a bit, and the front door opened. It was Akashi who opened the door.

"Anna!" He said and hugged me.

"Hey Akashi are you busy at the moment?"

"No why?"

"Want to come with me to the South Palace?"

"Yeah. Hang on, what's going on?"

"I just want to find out if King Jou knows anything about my parent's death."

"Wait what?"

"I want to find out if there is any record of my parent's death."

"Oh, I get what you mean now."

I smiled.

"Just wait here and I'll saddle my horse."

As I waited for Akashi to saddle his horse, I thought about Jai and that Akashi and I will probably see him while we are at the South Palace, it's not like he's not going to be there. Akashi rode out to me.

"You ready?"

"Yeah." I said and climbed on my own horse.

As we past the North markets Akashi started the conversation.

"So, what have you been up to?"

"At the moment I'm staying with May-Lyn."

"Nice" Akashi said. "So what about Kayato and his family?"

"Their staying there too."

"Cool, so where did Dean get to?"

"He is long gone."

"Oh okay."

We kept going until we got to the South Palace, we got off our horses. And we started walking to the front entrance.

"Anna, are you sure want to do this?" Akashi asked.

"Yes."

"Okay just making sure."

We walked to the front doors, Kanjo was on guard. "May I help you?" Kanjo said.

"We're here to see King Jou."

Kanjo opened the door and we walked in and we followed him, Kanjo led us down the first hallway and then the second and then around a corner and walked towards the wooden door, but today it wasn't guarded. Kanjo opened the door and we all walked in. King Jou was sitting on his throne, with Queen Rira. Standing next to King Jou was Prince Jai and that other woman, her hair was long and black. King Jou was talking to them. I looked at Akashi. He was calm. *What is her name?* Akashi held my hand, it didn't worry me, to Akashi and I holding hands is a sign of friendship, not boyfriend and girlfriend.

King Jou had stopped talking and Jai and the woman turned and faced us, as they past us I noticed that the woman had brown eyes and freckles. She smiled at me, I smiled back only for a second. Jai looked at Akashi's hand and mine. They kept walking.

"You're Highness." Kanjo said as the door closed behind Prince Jai and the woman.

"Yes Kanjo?" King Jou said.

"Anna would like to speak to you."

"Yes Anna."

"I would like to know if there is any record of my parent's death, Your Highness."

"I'll go and see." He said.

He got up and walked out of the room, a couple of minutes later he came back with a folder that read: Death Certificates. He flipped through until he got to O.

"Do you want me to check or would you like to do it yourself?"

"I'll do it."

Akashi let go of my hand and King Jou handed me the folder, I took it from him with both hands, and started to search for my last name which is O'Riley, I flipped through the pages carefully, but I couldn't find their name. *That's weird.* I handed the folder back to King Jou.

"Their death certificates are not in there." I told him.

"Okay." King Jou said slowly.

181

I turned and Akashi turned as well and we walked out the door, Kanjo opened the door for us, and we went back around the corner and down the second hallway and then the first, we were near the front entrance when:

"Anna." It was Prince Jai's voice.

"I'll be outside, Anna." Kanjo informed me.

"Okay."

Akashi and I turned to face Prince Jai, and he had the woman with him. The door closed behind Kanjo.

"Akashi this is Prince Jai."

"Nice to meet you Akashi." Prince Jai said.

"Nice to meet you You're Highness."

Akashi still had a hold of my hand.

"Anna, Akashi this is Princess Yuki." Jai introduced us.

"Nice to meet you both." She said.

I smiled and Akashi just stared, I noticed she had an engagement ring on her finger.

"How have you been Anna?" Prince Jai asked me.

"I have been good, and what about you Your Highness?"

"I have been well."

Akashi nudged me with his elbow.

"We better get going." I said.

"Please, stay for morning tea." Prince Jai said.

"Okay."

Prince Jai and Princess Yuki led the way; they were a few feet ahead of us.

"I'm not hungry." Akashi whispered to me.

"I'm not either, but we better eat something."

We walked along the first hallway and Prince Jai turned right and opened the door and we were in dining room. Queen Rira was already there, she sat on the far side and Jai sat beside her and Princess Yuki sat beside him, Akashi sat on the opposite side and I sat beside him, just then the door opened from the corner of my eye I saw King Jou, he sat down at the head of the table. Akashi and I sat drinking our tea. Akashi didn't eat much and neither did I.

After morning tea King Jou and Queen Rira went back to the throne room.

"Thank you for inviting us to morning tea Your Highness." I said to Prince Jai.

"Anytime Anna." Prince Jai said.

"We must get going, Kayato will be wondering where I got to."

Akashi held my hand and we walked to the front entrance, we got on our horses and took off to Akashi's house. After we got back to Akashi's house we rode up to the stables.

"Are you okay?" Akashi asked.

"Yep. I'll see you around, Akashi."

"Bye Anna." Akashi said.

I turned my horse around and headed to the North Palace, on my way back to the North Palace a hundred metres in front of me I saw the behind of a grey horse. *King Daichi? No it can't be he said that he would be back this afternoon.* I made my horse break into a trot. I kept going until I got to the North Palace, I took my horse straight to the stables; Akio was still there, he was brushing May-Lyn's horse, I got off mine.

"Excuse me Akio."

"Yes Anna?" He looked me.

"Where's May-Lyn and Ema?"

Akio didn't seem surprised when I didn't call May-Lyn by her full name which is Princess May-Lyn.

"Her Highness and Ema are in the courtyard, they have a visitor with them." Akio answered me.

"Thanks." I said.

I walked from the stables and crept along the side of the North Palace, as I got to the corner I shuffled back the way I came only for a foot, then I peered around the side. May-Lyn, Ema and the visitor had their back to me, which was good. I quickly walked back along the side and to the front entrance of the Palace. I opened the door and quickly walked in. *I'm so stupid the visitor is Prince Jai!* I decided to not go out to the courtyard. If Prince Jai wants to speak with me he has to find me. I didn't know what to do now so I decided to go to the dining room and sit down; I walked to my left and quickly walked to the door and opened it. I sat at the seat I had sat in at breakfast. *Why is Prince Jai here?* Just then the door opened.

"Anna." It was Kayato.

"Yes Kayato?" I said without turning to face him.

He walked up to a chair and sat down beside me. "We're heading back to my house after lunch."

"Okay."

"Do you know that Prince Jai is here?" Kayato asked.

"Yes."

"He bumped into me, and he said that he would like to talk to you."

"What about?" I asked.

"He didn't say."

I sighed. I don't want to know what Prince Jai has to tell me. Just then we heard a whimper I looked behind me to find Snowbell standing in the room and looking at me, I got up and picked up Snowbell and headed outside. At the front entrance of the North Palace was some grass, I sat on the left side away from the entrance and put Snowbell down on the grass with me. I patted her.

"Hey girl, have you been good" I said as I ruffled her hair.

I noticed somebody standing at the right side of the entrance; I looked up and saw Prince Jai. *Great, now he sees me talking to the dog, he probably thinks I'm insane.* I quickly looked back at Snowbell she barked and then sat down next to me. I didn't know what to do now so I just sat there looking at the ground. I decided to go back inside.

"Come on Snowbell." I said as I got up and started walking towards the doors.

I walked inside and bounded up the stairs to the bathroom, once I got to the bathroom I quickly washed my hands and went back down the steps to the dining room. *I bet Prince Jai will be in there.* I opened the door and only May-Lyn and Ema were sitting in the dining room. They had their backs to me, I sat next to Ema, and they weren't talking like they usually were. I noticed that there were four bowls of rice on the side that we were sitting on and the other side had six.

"Hey." I said.

"Hey." They both said at the same time.

Just then the door opened, and Queen Miranda sat on the opposite side to May-Lyn.

"Hello ladies." Queen Miranda said.

"Hello mother." May-Lyn said.

"You're Highness." Ema and I said.

Again the door opened. Yasumi sat next to Queen Miranda, Monikku sat next to her mother and Kayato sat on the left side of Monikku then Taro and Emika. I nearly jumped out of my chair when Prince Jai sat beside me; I wasn't expecting him to do that. While I ate I noticed that I was shaking. *Come on Anna, focus.* I gripped my chopsticks firmly. I had my right hand under the table and Jai held my hand and lightly squeezed my hand. *Why is he doing this?*

After lunch Jai let go of my hand, I bounded towards the stairs; May-Lyn and Ema were outside. I thought I better get changed back into my purple kimono. I dashed to the guest bedroom and went to the wardrobe and took out my purple kimono and quickly got changed and put the yellow kimono back on my bed, I got the other kimonos and put them on the bed also, I put my sword on. I then walked out of the room and closed the door behind me, and headed down the stairs and walked towards the front doors, I was about halfway to the doors when:

"Anna." Jai's voice said.

I stopped walking and looked to my left and there he was standing. "You're Highness." I replied and kept walking to the front doors.

I opened them and walked out; May-Lyn and Ema were standing with my horse. I walked towards them. I patted his blazer.

"I'll come and visit." May-Lyn said and hugged me.

"May, I can't breathe." I said.

She let go of me and it was Ema's turn to hug me.

"See you soon, Anna."

"You sure will." I said.

Just then Kayato and Taro came from the stables on their horses. I climbed on my horse, and Jai came from the stables on his horse. We took off and headed to Kayato's house. *Where are Yasumi, Monikku and Emika?* Maybe they headed back already. I didn't say anything, Kayato and Taro were in front and Jai and I were at the back. Jai moved his horse closer to mine, as we past the markets Kayato and Taro made their horses break into a canter. I kept my horse at the trot so did Jai, if he wants his horse to canter it wouldn't worry me. After a bit we finally came to Kayato's house, Jai followed. We got off our horses and Shi-Lou and Jin took our horses. Even Prince Jai's horse, just then Monikku came out to the front veranda and bolted down the steps.

"Taro!" She said happily.

"Whoa, hey slow down." He said as he hugged his little sister.

Taro put Monikku down and they walked up the front steps and they walked inside, Kayato walked in after them, I followed Kayato and Jai followed me. I walked along the hallway and I led Jai around the corner and we were in the lounge room, I decided to go out on the back veranda, Jai followed. I noticed Taro and Emika were sitting in the lounge room with Monikku, she had Snowbell with her. Kayato and Yasumi entered the room from the kitchen. I opened the door and walked to the round table and sat down, Jai closed the door behind him and sat down next to me.

"Kayato said you would like to talk to me." I said looking at Jai.

"I'm engaged." He said.

It felt like I had no air in my lungs. Jai continued talking:

"The other night when you saw me at the South Beach, you weren't meant to see me kissing her."

"But I did Jai, I saw it."

"I know and I'm sorry." He said.

"Were you going to tell me about her" I asked him.

"I was going to tell you that night when I was at the beach with her, but we saw you there, and you were walking off and you were crying, and I thought if I went to visit you after you saw us kissing that you might not want to talk to me."

"So you don't hate me?" I asked.

His eyes were confused. "No I don't hate you."

I sighed in relief. "Because the other day when Dean and I were at the North Markets and he kissed me, I didn't want to kiss him so I pulled away" I paused. "And I went after you and I called out to you, but you were already on your horse." I informed him.

He didn't say anything, I walked down the steps and made my way over to the stone wall and sat down, I looked straight in front of me to where a cherry blossom tree was. Just then Jai came down the steps, I didn't look, and he sat beside me and put his arm around my lower back and pulled me close to him. I just looked at the cherry blossom tree.

"Anna." Jai said.

I didn't say anything, I had nothing to say.

"Anna?" He said a second time.

"Yes?" I said. I closed my eyes for a second and opened them and a tear came rushing out and another and another.

"I do love you, but the marriage is an arrangement, by Princess Yuki's mother."

I cried more, he put his left arm around my stomach and he linked his fingers together.

"How long have you been engaged to her?" I asked as I sobbed.

"That night when you saw us kissing at the beach." He answered my question.

I tried to fight the tears but they wouldn't stop, he hugged me tighter. I wanted to kiss him so bad but I better not.

"Won't Princess Yuki get jealous?" I asked.

"No." Prince Jai said bluntly.

Jai unwrapped his hands, I stood and started to walk back to the house, but Jai grabbed my hand.

"Anna."

"Go home Jai." I said to him without looking at him.

I pulled my hand away from his and kept walking; I wiped the tears away from my eyes and face. I rushed up the steps and walked straight to my bedroom I put my sword in its case and lied down on my bed and I lied on my right side, I had my left leg on top of my right leg, I brought my legs near me and I wrapped my arms around my legs and fell asleep.

It was night when I woke up, my body was in a totally different position to when I fell asleep, my hands were on the pillow and my head was lying in between them. I got up slowly and went to the bathroom. I then went to the kitchen, I checked the time it was 6:15 pm. I sighed, and then walked out to the back veranda and sat down. *When Jai was at the North Palace, I bet that's what he was telling May-Lyn and Ema, that he is engaged. So that's why they were quiet at lunch time today.* Just then Emika came out and sat beside me.

"Jai is engaged." I blurted out.

"Are you okay?" Emika asked.

"I have to be, don't I?" I answered her.

"I see the way Prince Jai looks at you, he does love you" Emika said. "Have you met Jai's fiancée?"

"Yes, Jai introduced Akashi and me to her when we went there to see King Jou about my parent's death certificates."

We got up and walked inside and sat down at the kitchen table, while we ate dinner I was thinking of a plan. *If I wake up early next morning pack my back-pack with some clothes and grab my toiletry bag and saddle my horse and take off to my Grandparent's house and also leave a note/letter for Kayato to tell him what's going on.* I decided on that and if that didn't work just saddle my horse and take off. It was after dinner and I dashed off to the bathroom to have a shower and to clean my teeth, I decided to leave my toiletry bag in the bathroom until tomorrow morning, if I took it out now someone is bound to notice that I'm up to something. I grabbed a piece of paper and a pen and went to the kitchen.

As I made my way out to the kitchen they were all sitting down.

I walked back to my bedroom and decided to leave it for tomorrow morning. I put the pen and paper on the bed side table I grabbed the letters that Jai had wrote to me and the copy of the letter of Akashi's I then walked to the wardrobe and pulled out my luggage and opened it and sat down on the floor, I put the letters on the right side of me and fished through the clothes until I found my back-pack. I rested it on my left thigh and opened it, I pulled out my photo album, good thing it wasn't very big, I opened it and picked up the letters and put them in there then I quickly put that in my back-pack and I then picked out some clothes and folded them and put them in my back-pack, I closed the back-pack up, closed up my luggage bag and put that back in the wardrobe and I grabbed my back-pack and sat that on top of the luggage bag. I got into the bed; I took off my locket and placed it on the bedside table.

I woke early next morning, I dashed to the wardrobe and grabbed any kimono and my back-pack and sat it on my bed and went to the bathroom to get changed and to clean my teeth, I grabbed my toiletry bag and made my way back to my bedroom I put the toiletry bag in the back-pack, I put my back-pack on my back I put my sword on and also my locket and then I got the piece of paper and the pen and went to the kitchen table. As I made my way down the hallway to the kitchen I was hoping no one was up yet, I walked into the kitchen and made sure I didn't step on the floor board that went creak. I sat down at the kitchen table and started to write:

To Kayato

I want to thank you for being my teacher for the past seven months; you're probably wondering why I'm writing this to you. I'm writing this to you because I'm not living with you and your family anymore, I know this is short notice but I decided last night that I can't stay here with everything that has happen over the past couple of days. Please tell your family that I say goodbye and that I'm sorry for leaving like this. I wish I could explain but I can't. I will be staying at my Grandparents house.

From Anna.

I folded the letter and wrote Kayato on it, and took off my back-pack and put the pen in then I quickly shut it and put it back on my back, I walked to door that led out to the back veranda, I shut it behind me and hurried down the steps to the stables.

"Hey Coco." I said and patted his blazer.

I undid the stable door and walked in and grabbed my riding gear and saddled him, I then led him out of the stables, I shut the stable door and then I climbed on and rode off to my Grandparent's house.

As their house came into view I made my horse break into a canter, I went to the stables Grandpa probably would be up, as I made my way down to the stables I saw Grandpa emptying a bucket of water. As my horse got closer he turned around to see who it was.

"Anna." Grandpa said.

I got off my horse and walked up to him and hugged him. "Hey" I said after I hugged him. "Is it okay if I stay with you and Grandma for a while?"

"Anna, you know you can stay with us anytime." He answered me.

I smiled and unsaddled my horse, and Grandpa took him out into the paddock with some of the other horses and then we made our way up to the house.

To be continued . . .

Acknowledgments

I would like to thank my sister Emma for giving brilliant ideas, to my parents and Grandmother, The team at Author House UK, you guys are the best.